Thinking o...

Clint knew trouble was coming, and he hoped that Baron Giles was up to the task. It looked as if all five men were going to try drawing on him. He was going to have to take Feathers first and then Cuddy—but he recalled what Giles had said about Feathers, about him rushing his shots.

Cuddy first, he decided, then Feathers.

At least, he hoped it was the right decision . . .

DON'T MISS THESE
ALL-ACTION WESTERN SERIES
FROM THE BERKLEY PUBLISHING GROUP

THE GUNSMITH by J. R. Roberts
Clint Adams was a legend among lawmen, outlaws, and ladies. They called him . . . the Gunsmith.

LONGARM by Tabor Evans
The popular long-running series about Deputy U.S. Marshal Custis Long—his life, his loves, his fight for justice.

SLOCUM by Jake Logan
Today's longest-running action Western. John Slocum rides a deadly trail of hot blood and cold steel.

BUSHWHACKERS by B. J. Lanagan
An action-packed series by the creators of Longarm! The rousing adventures of the most brutal gang of cutthroats ever assembled—Quantrill's Raiders.

DIAMONDBACK by Guy Brewer
Dex Yancey is Diamondback, a Southern gentleman turned con man when his brother cheats him out of the family fortune. Ladies love him. Gamblers hate him. But nobody pulls one over on Dex . . .

WILDGUN by Jack Hanson
The blazing adventures of mountain man Will Barlow—from the creators of Longarm!

TEXAS TRACKER by Tom Calhoun
J. T. Law: the most relentless—and dangerous—manhunter in all Texas. Where sheriffs and posses fail, he's the best man to bring in the most vicious outlaws—for a price.

THE GUNSMITH

315

THE MADAME OF SILVER JUNCTION

J. R. ROBERTS

JOVE BOOKS, NEW YORK

THE BERKLEY PUBLISHING GROUP
Published by the Penguin Group
Penguin Group (USA) Inc.
375 Hudson Street, New York, New York 10014, USA
Penguin Group (Canada), 90 Eglinton Avenue East, Suite 700, Toronto, Ontario M4P 2Y3, Canada
(a division of Pearson Penguin Canada Inc.)
Penguin Books Ltd., 80 Strand, London WC2R 0RL, England
Penguin Group Ireland, 25 St. Stephen's Green, Dublin 2, Ireland (a division of Penguin Books Ltd.)
Penguin Group (Australia), 250 Camberwell Road, Camberwell, Victoria 3124, Australia
(a division of Pearson Australia Group Pty. Ltd.)
Penguin Books India Pvt. Ltd., 11 Community Centre, Panchsheel Park, New Delhi—110 017, India
Penguin Group (NZ), 67 Apollo Drive, Rosedale, North Shore 0632, New Zealand
(a division of Pearson New Zealand Ltd.)
Penguin Books (South Africa) (Pty.) Ltd., 24 Sturdee Avenue, Rosebank, Johannesburg 2196,
South Africa

Penguin Books Ltd., Registered Offices: 80 Strand, London WC2R 0RL, England

This is a work of fiction. Names, characters, places, and incidents either are the product of the author's imagination or are used fictitiously, and any resemblance to actual persons, living or dead, business establishments, events, or locales is entirely coincidental.

THE MADAME OF SILVER JUCNTION

A Jove Book / published by arrangement with the author

PRINTING HISTORY
Jove edition / March 2008

ISBN: 978-0-515-14427-7

JOVE®
Jove Books are published by The Berkley Publishing Group,
a division of Penguin Group (USA) Inc.,
375 Hudson Street, New York, New York 10014.
JOVE is a registered trademark of Penguin Group (USA) Inc.
The "J" design is a trademark belonging to Penguin Group (USA) Inc.

PRINTED IN THE UNITED STATES OF AMERICA

10 9 8 7 6 5 4 3 2 1

ONE

Clint didn't pass a signpost that would give him an idea of the size of Silver Junction, Nevada. But as he rode in, it had the look and feel of a town that was definitely experiencing growing pains. The streets were alive with people going about their business, giving him hardly a look as he rode in. The buildings were a mixture of new and old, and here and there he saw banners asking the town to VOTE FOR DONNER, or EXNER FOR MAYOR, or VOTE FOR PROPOSITION 3. Lots of activity, new buildings, new government, always the sign of a town on the rise.

He was glad that Juliet had found her way here to start her long-planned business. He'd met her several years ago when, in her late twenties, she had come West to start over. Back then she'd been working in a restaurant in St. Joe, Missouri, waiting tables. She was pretty enough to be a saloon girl, but she'd had no desire to break into that business. She certainly had the talent in the bedroom to be a whore, but that hadn't been on her list of possible careers, either.

They had only spent a few days together, but beyond enjoying each other in bed they had become friends. She told him that when she finally got her business up and running she'd let him know and he could come and see her.

Now it had been a few weeks since he'd received her telegram in Labyrinth, Texas, and he felt bad that it had taken him this long to get here. He'd headed this way more than once, but, as usually happened, he'd gotten himself involved in something that wasn't really his business, and it had taken up a good portion of his time. His friend Rick Hartman asked him time and again why he was such a soft touch for people who needed help. Clint's reply was always the same—what else did he have to do?

Clint traveled a lot, but never really with a destination in mind. And when he wasn't traveling, he was sitting in Rick's saloon in Labyrinth. Anyone else with that much time on their hands might even claim to be retired. But Clint had nothing to be retired from. He couldn't very well retire from being the Gunsmith, because that would mean putting down his gun—and that would mean being dead five minutes later. That was the hand he'd been dealt years ago, and that was the hand he had to play.

He rode past several saloons, and wondered if one of them was Juliet's new business. Had she ended up going that way? Or did she own one of the small restaurants he rode by? He was about to ask directions to the nearest livery when he spotted it at the end of a small side street. He directed Eclipse, his Darley Arabian, to the livery, fairly sure he would not discover that this was Juliet's new venture.

He dismounted in front and walked the animal inside. As usual, the liveryman was impressed by the animal. Clint was used to this, and knew that most of the men he came in contact with would take good care of the horse.

After he negotiated a price for at least a few days, he grabbed his saddlebags and rifle and left. While passing several hotels, he'd picked out the one he liked and walked back to it.

The desk clerk was effusive, to say the least. A dapper man with a bow tie and slicked-down hair parted in the center.

"Ah, a stranger in town. Welcome to Silver Junction, sir. Can I offer you a room?"

"For free?" Clint asked.

"Ah, well, no, what I meant was—"

"Yes, I'll take a room for a few days."

"Excellent," the man said. "Please sign the register."

He turned the book, and Clint wrote down his real name.

"I'm sure you were joking with me, sir. I'm afraid I haven't got much of a sense of humor. I apologize—"

"There's no need for that," Clint said. "I'll take my key."

"Of course, of course, Mr.—" The clerk stopped, turned the book around and read the name. "Mr. . . . Clint Adams?"

"That's right."

"Yes, sir," the man said stammering. "R-right away, s-sir. Your key." He handed it to Clint. "Room four, sir. Best in the house."

"Thanks."

"Uh, anything I can do for you, sir, just let me know."

"No, there's nothing—" Clint started, then stopped and said, "Maybe there is something. Do you know a woman named Juliet Fuller?"

"Um . . . Fuller, did you say?"

"Yes, Juliet."

"No, um, I'm afraid I don't, s-sir," the man said.

Clint wasn't sure if the man was lying, or if it was just his nerves. He decided not to push it.

"All right, then," Clint said. "Thanks for the room."

"Yes, sir," the clerk said. "E-enjoy your stay."

"I'll try."

TWO

The room was satisfactory, as good as any he'd had recently in a Western hotel. The building itself was one of the newer ones in town. He went to the window and looked down at the main street, which was bustling with as much if not more activity as when he first rode in to town. It was nearing three, probably the height of business in any town. He decided to go right out and see if he could find Juliet's business. Her telegram had indicated that she was deliberately leaving him in the dark. "What I am doing is for me to know and you to find out," it had said.

He left the room.

After Clint had gone up to his room, the nervous desk clerk ran from the lobby into the street, where he was almost run over by a buckboard.

"Watch where ya goin', ya idiot!" the driver shouted.

The clerk waved, then continued on across the street, then down to the next block where he came upon his destination—the sheriff's office.

As he burst into the office, Sheriff Walt Sheldon looked up from his desk.

"What the hell are you doin', Andy?" Sheldon demanded.

"Sheriff, you'll never guess who just checked into the hotel," Andy Wills said breathlessly.

"You're right, Andy," he said, "I never will, because I'm not even gonna try. You're just gonna tell me."

"Clint Adams."

Sheldon frowned at the hotel clerk.

"The Gunsmith?"

"That's right."

"Here in Silver Junction?"

"That's what I'm tellin' you!"

"What's he doin' here?"

"I wasn't about to ask him any questions," Andy said. "He'd just as soon shoot me as look at me. He's one mean son of a bitch, Sheriff, I'm tellin' you."

"Andy," Sheldon said, "you wouldn't be tryin' to shine me on, would you?"

"I swear, Sheriff, he's there," Andy said. "And that ain't all."

"Whataya mean, that ain't all?"

Andy leaned in and lowered his voice, even though they were the only two people in the office.

"He was askin' after that gal."

"What gal?"

"You know . . . that gal? That Juliet gal?"

"Is that a fact? Exactly what was he askin'?"

"Just if I knew her."

"And what did you say?"

"I said no."

"You lied to him."

"Well—"

"He's gonna find out you knew her, Andy," Sheriff Sheldon said. "Hell, we all knew 'er."

Suddenly, it hit Andy and his eyes grew wide.

"He's gonna kill me, ain't he?"

"Relax," Sheldon said. "I'll take care of it."

"You gonna kill him?"

"Nobody's gonna kill nobody," the sheriff said. "I'm just gonna have a talk with him, find out what his interest is, that's all."

"What should I do?"

"Just go on back to work."

"With the Gunsmith on the loose?"

"He ain't on the loose, Andy," Sheldon said. "He ain't done nothin'. He's got every right to check in to a hotel. Just don't be scared, and don't lie to him anymore."

"Are you sure about this?" Andy asked. "I don't wanna get shot dead, Sheriff."

"I told you," the sheriff said impatiently, "nobody's gettin' shot. Just get back to work."

"When are you gonna talk to him?"

"I don't know, Andy," Sheldon said. "As soon as I get a chance. Now go!"

Hesitantly, Andy made his way to the door and then, with a deep breath, went out.

As he left the hotel, Clint noticed the desk clerk was not there. He didn't have long to wonder where the man had gone. As he was walking down the street, he saw him coming out of the sheriff's office. It was a pretty safe bet that the local law now knew he was in town.

THREE

Clint took a walk around town, stopped into certain businesses—a hat store, a dress shop, a confectionary—and did not find Juliet in any of them. He finally decided to stop at a saloon for a beer and chose a place called the Fatted Calf Saloon. It was small, with only about half a dozen tables and a short bar. It was also apparently not a popular place, as there was only one man standing at the bar, and one other seated at a table—this at a time when most saloons would be filling up.

"Beer," he told the bartender.

"Comin' up."

When the man came back with a beer, Clint asked, "Do you know a woman named Juliet Fuller?" He figured bartenders knew everybody in town.

"Not my business," the bartender said.

"I'm only asking if you know—"

"I only know people who come through those doors," the barman said, pointing.

"So you're saying she never came through those doors?" Clint asked.

"That's what I'm sayin'."

"Then you do know her," Clint went on, "she's just never come in here."

"I ain't sayin' no more," the bartender said.

At that moment the batwings allowed two more men to enter. They walked to the bar and the bartender went to serve them.

The lone man at the bar said to Clint in a low voice, "If I was you, I'd talk to the sheriff."

"What?"

The man didn't look at him, just said, "Talk to the sheriff."

Clint wanted to ask more questions, but it seemed as if the man didn't want anyone to know he was talking. So Clint finished his beer and left the saloon.

Sheriff Walt Sheldon was standing outside the Fatted Calf when Clint Adams came walking out. The sheriff didn't know what he looked like, but the Gunsmith was the only stranger in town that he had heard of. He'd seen the man duck into the Calf and had decided to stand outside and wait for him.

"Clint Adams?" he asked as the Gunsmith came out.

Clint stopped, stared, and said, "That's right."

Sheldon moved his leather vest aside so Clint could see the badge pinned to his shirt.

"Well," Clint said, "I was just about to come looking for you, Sheriff."

"That a fact? I don't suppose you'd give me your gun if I asked for it," the lawman said.

"You got a reason to ask for it?"

"Just in the interest of avoiding trouble."

"Believe me, Sheriff," Clint said. "After all these years

I avoid more trouble by wearing it than by not wearing it, so no, I wouldn't give it to you."

"Why don't we take a walk to my office so we can talk in private."

"That's fine with me," Clint said.

"This way."

Clint followed the man to his office.

"About all I got I can offer you is coffee," the sheriff said, indicating the pot atop a cast-iron stove.

"Strong?"

"I usually use it to clean my badge."

"Then I'll take a cup."

Sheldon went to the stove, poured two cups, handed one to Clint, and went around to seat himself behind his desk. Clint took the chair in front of the desk.

"What brings you to my town, Mr. Adams?"

"I'm here to see a friend."

"And what friend would that be?"

"A woman named Juliet Fuller," Clint said. "Do you know who she is?"

"I know who she is."

"That's good," Clint said, "because nobody in town will admit to knowing her. Makes me kind of suspicious."

"Well then, I guess what I have to tell you will make you even more suspicious."

"And what's that?"

The lawman hesitated, then said, "I'm afraid your friend, Juliet Fuller, is dead."

FOUR

"How did she die?"

"She was killed."

"Killed?" Clint asked. "There are lots of ways to get killed, Sheriff."

"Uh, she was murdered."

"When?"

"Last week."

"Do you have the killer?"

"No."

"Do you know who it is?"

"No."

"Why not?"

"Look at me, Mr. Adams," Sheldon said. "I'm a sheriff, not a detective."

"How was she murdered?"

"Somebody strangled her."

"Where?"

"Her place."

"Her house? Her place of business?"

"Same thing. Do you, uh, know what she was doin' for a livin', Mr. Adams?"

"No," Clint said. "I got a telegram telling me she'd opened a business here and I'd find out what kind when I got here. What kind of business was it?"

"She was running the local whorehouse."

"That can't be."

"Why not?"

"She wasn't a whore."

"Well, I didn't say she was a whore," Sheldon said. "I said she was runnin' the place."

"Like a madam, you mean?"

"I guess that's what you'd call it," the lawman said.

"Was this the only whorehouse in town?"

"It was."

"And is it still open and operating?"

"It, uh, is."

"By who? Did she have a partner?"

"There was no partner that I know of," the sheriff said.

"Then who's running it now?"

"A man named Lincoln Town."

"And what was his connection to Juliet? Or the business?" Clint asked.

"None."

"Then why is he running it?"

"He just . . . stepped in."

"And you let him?"

"If it wasn't for him, the place would have closed and those women would be out of jobs. Or out on the streets."

"Did it ever occur to you that he might have killed her in order to take over her business?"

"Actually, no," the man said, "it didn't."

"Then you're right, Sheriff."

"About what?"

"You're no detective."

They talked a little while longer, but Clint was not getting any satisfaction from the man.

"So you're telling me nobody in this town cares that she was killed?" Clint asked. "Nobody in this town is trying to find out who did it?"

"She only came to town last month," the sheriff said, as if that was an excuse. "Nobody knew her real well. I'm afraid she didn't have many friends here."

"So it's okay that somebody killed her?"

"No, but—"

"So she was killed where, in a house? Where she lived and worked?"

"That's right."

"Where is it."

"Why?"

"I want to have a look," Clint said. "I want to talk to the girls who worked for her."

"Look," the sheriff said, "if you go over there, there's gonna be trouble."

"Between me and who? This Lincoln Town?"

"I don't think he'll like—"

"I don't think he'll like what I'm going to do, either," Clint said, cutting the lawman off.

"Why? What are you gonna do?" Sheldon asked.

Clint grinned without any humor and said, "I'm going to kick his ass out of there."

FIVE

"That won't be an easy thing," the sheriff said, "even for you."

"Is he a hard man?"

Sheldon nodded and said, "And he's got more hard men workin' for him."

"So that's why he was able to move in on her business as soon as she was dead," Clint said. "Does this town have a judge?"

"It does, but he won't make a ruling on that."

"Maybe a federal judge would."

"That'd be up to you, I guess," the lawman said. "But if I was you, I wouldn't let word leak out that you're thinkin' of bringin' federal help in here."

"Is that a threat, or a warning?"

"That's a warning, Mr. Adams," Sheldon said. "I don't make threats."

"Well," Clint said, standing, "thanks for your time, Sheriff."

"Are you plannin' on stayin' in town?" the sheriff asked, as he also stood.

"Oh, yeah"

"How long?"

"Just until I find out who killed Juliet."

"You ain't gonna let it go, then?"

"No, Sheriff," Clint said, "I'm not going to let it go."

The sheriff walked with Clint to the door of the office.

"What was your connection to Miss Fuller?"

"We were friends."

"Sweethearts?"

"Friends, Sheriff," Clint said, again, "and I don't take kindly to people killing my friends."

"Well, just be on the lookout when you talk to Town," Sheldon said.

"For anyone in particular?"

The sheriff hesitated, then said, "Yeah, he's got a fella named Cuddy workin' for him, Frank Cuddy. Handy fella with a gun."

"Just handy?"

"Real handy."

"I've never heard of him."

"He's kinda young," Sheldon said, "hasn't made a name for himself yet. He finds out you're in town, though, he might take that as an opportunity."

"Thanks," Clint said, "I'll keep that in mind."

Sheldon opened the door.

"Look," he said, "I've been sheriff here for a few years. I'll be forty next year. I'd like to live to see that birthday."

"Meaning what?"

"Meaning don't make me do anythin' that's gonna get me killed," the lawman said. "I don't have any deputies, so whatever comes up I got to handle myself."

"I tell you what, Sheriff," Clint said. "Whatever I do, I'll pretty much be handling it myself."

"Good intentions," Sheriff Sheldon said. "They scare me the most."

SIX

Clint followed directions given to him by the sheriff and realized he'd passed the house earlier in the day. It was a big old house, two stories high and well cared for. Juliet had always said if she got her own business she'd be sure to take care of it. He wondered how she had gotten the money to buy herself this house, and how she had come to turn it into a whorehouse. She had never even wanted to work in a saloon.

He mounted the front steps and knocked on the front door. It was after four in the afternoon. A whorehouse would certainly be open for business. He was about to knock a second time when the heavy wooden door opened, leaving a woman standing in the doorway. She had a robe on, and pulled it tight around her body as she folded her arms across her chest. Her hair was done up, and she'd obviously been working on her makeup.

"Come back at five o'clock, cowboy," she said. "We ain't open just yet."

"That's okay," Clint said, "I'm not buying what you're selling."

"Mister," she said, "you ain't even seen what I'm sellin'.

If you did, you'd be buyin'." She dropped her hands and took hold of the robe as if to open it. "You want a sneak peek?"

"That's okay," he said. "Keep your robe closed. I just want to talk to someone."

"That's gonna cost you the same," she said, "and you still gotta come back at five."

"Is Mr. Town here?"

She made a face that made it very clear what she thought of Mr. Town and said, "No, he ain't."

"I want to talk to someone about Juliet Fuller."

"Juliet?" The girl frowned. "She's dead."

"I know."

"Did you know her?"

"I did," he answered. "We were friends. I came here to see her. I didn't like finding out that she's dead."

"None of us like it."

"That's good," he said. "I'd like to talk to someone who knew her."

"We all knew her."

"How many girls work here?"

"Nine."

"Are they all here now?"

"Yeah."

"Then I'd like to come in and talk to all of you."

"Some of them are asleep."

"What do you say we wake them up?" he asked.

She thought a moment, then smiled and said, "Why not?"

Within fifteen minutes Clint was in the whorehouse drawing room with ten women, varying in age from seventeen to forty. "Juliet always said it was good to have a variety on hand." That was Regina, the girl who had answered the door. For the moment, that was the only name he thought he needed to remember.

"Girls," Regina said, "this is Clint Adams. He says he was a friend of Juliet's. Does anyone remember her mentioning him?"

"I do," a woman who looked forty said. She had dark hair with a small streak of gray, and a full body that was just beginning to get a little too full.

"So do I," called out a thirtyish redhead, who was tall and slender, with long hair worn in a ponytail. "She talked very highly of him."

"That's what I was going to say," the other woman chimed in. She looked at Clint. "You must be so devastated to find that she's dead."

Clint didn't know what Juliet had told these women about their relationship. He was upset that she was dead because they had been friends, but he wasn't *devastated*. This woman obviously thought that they had been much more than friends. Clint wondered if that meant that Juliet had thought so, too.

"I am," he replied. "I'm very upset. I want to know who killed her."

The older woman made a rude noise and said, "We pretty much all know that."

"Louisa," Regina said warningly.

"Come on, Reggie," Louisa said. "Everybody knows it and nobody's saying anything."

"It was Lincoln," the redhead said. "Lincoln Town. It had to be. He killed her."

"Oh, I don't think he did it himself," Louisa said, "but he had it done. Probably by his trained mongrel."

"Frank Cuddy?" Clint asked.

"You know about him, already?" Louisa asked.

"I do," Clint said.

Louisa looked around the room with a smile and said, "Girls, we may just have the answer to all our prayers standing right here in the room with us."

SEVEN

Clint decided that he really only needed to talk with Louisa and the redhead, Ginger. He told the other girls they could leave and remained in the drawing room with Louisa, Ginger, and Regina, who insisted on staying.

"I let him in," she explained to the other two girls. "I'm responsible."

Clint got the distinct feeling that Louisa and Ginger did not get along with Regina, but he let it go.

"First of all," he said, "I didn't know what Juliet's business here in town was. She sent me a telegram, but didn't give me any specifics."

"She said you'd be shocked," Louisa said. "But she also said that when she explained the details to you, you'd understand."

"She said you were a very understanding man," Ginger added.

"Among other things." Louisa smirked.

"I take it you two girls were the closest to her?" Clint asked.

"Louisa came here with Juliet," Ginger said. "I was

hired later, but we really hit it off. We only knew each other a month, but she was my best friend."

"She was your boss," Regina pointed out.

"She still was my best friend."

Regina rolled her eyes.

"Do I smell coffee?" Clint asked.

"There's always a pot on in the kitchen," Ginger said. "Juliet said you liked it strong, and you'd appreciate that it was always available. I can get you some, if you like."

She started to rise but Clint waved her back down.

"No, I still have some questions for you," Clint said. "Regina, could I have a cup of coffee? Would you mind?"

Regina looked at them all, then said, "Oh, all right. I'll get it for you."

As she left the room, Clint leaned forward and said, "Tell me about Regina."

"She works for Lincoln," Louisa said. "She and Juliet didn't get along."

"Juliet was going to fire her as soon as she found another girl," Ginger said.

"So she'll report everything we say back to Lincoln Town?" Clint asked.

"Without a doubt," Louisa said.

"When I answered the door and asked for him, I got the feeling Regina didn't like him."

"She doesn't," Louisa said, "but he likes her, and she knows how to play men. With Juliet dead, her job is safe."

"In fact," Ginger said, "she expects him to make her Juliet's replacement."

"As madam?' Clint asked.

"Hostess," Louisa said. "Juliet said she was the hostess."

"All right," Clint said.

"Is that why you asked her to get you coffee?" Ginger asked. "To get her out of the room?"

"Yes," he said, "now I know where she stands."

"Juliet always said you were smart," Ginger commented.

"Among other things," Louisa said again.

Clint leaned back and Regina reentered the room holding a mug of coffee.

"Thank you," he said, taking it from her. She sat back down and looked at them all expectantly.

"Why don't you girls tell me why you think Lincoln Town had Juliet killed?" he asked.

EIGHT

Regina sat and listened carefully while Louisa and Ginger talked with Clint about Lincoln Town.

"He wanted Juliet from the time she arrived in town," Louisa told him. "And when she made it clear he couldn't have her, he decided he wanted this place."

"Even before it opened?"

"Lincoln knew a whorehouse would do well in Silver Junction," Ginger said.

"Did you know him before?" Clint asked.

"Yes," she said. "I worked in some of the saloons in town before Juliet hired me."

"After a week we knew this place was a gold mine," Louisa said. "So did Lincoln. He made her several offers and she refused each one. He got more and more angry."

"So you think he decided to have her killed and then move right in."

"And that's exactly what happened," Ginger said.

"It's just a coincidence," Regina said.

They all turned their heads and looked at her.

"Do you really think so?" Clint asked.

"He wouldn't do something like that."

"You just want to make sure you keep your job here," Ginger said.

"He had Cuddy do it," Louisa said. "I know it."

"Maybe Cuddy did do it," Regina admitted, "but it wasn't on Lincoln's word."

"Where would I find Mr. Lincoln Town?" Clint asked.

"He's got an office in town," Louisa said. "Above a saloon called the Pat Hand."

"Is he a gambler?"

"Among other things," Ginger said.

"He's a businessman," Regina said.

Louisa looked at Clint and said, "Yeah, among other things."

It was Regina who walked Clint to the door. He told Louisa and Ginger he'd be back to talk to them further.

"You can't listen to those two," Regina said, at the door.

"Why not?"

"They disliked Lincoln from the start."

"That's funny."

"What is?"

"When I first asked for him at the door, I had the feeling you didn't like him much, either."

Her eyes darted around, as if she were checking to see if anybody had heard Clint.

"No, no," she said, "that's not the case at all. I-I like him fine. He's my boss."

"Just because he's your boss doesn't mean you have to like him, Regina."

"I like him fine, I said!"

"Okay, you like him fine," Clint said. "I'll tell anyone who asks that you said so."

"Mister," Regina said, "you're lookin' for trouble."

"I'm looking for the man who had my friend killed, Regina," he said. "He's the one who's looking for trouble."

NINE

Clint left the whorehouse and walked back to the center of town. He remembered passing the Pat Hand on the way in. He'd already tabbed it as the place he'd go if he wanted to find a poker game.

When the end of the workday approached, the street traffic started to thin out as people headed home or into the saloons. Clint approached the Pat Hand and could hear voices and piano music coming from inside. As he got closer, he could hear another familiar sound—poker chips. If they were using chips, then the Pat Hand was a serious gambling establishment. Did Lincoln Town think that Juliet's whorehouse would make a nice addition to his holdings? Or was he just looking to get it away from her because she had rebuffed his advances?

Clint mounted the boardwalk and approached the batwing doors, thinking that he already had a good idea what kind of man Lincoln Town was—the kind who didn't like to be told no.

He entered the place, pausing just inside to take a look. It was a big room doing a big business. There were girls working the floor and gaming tables of all kinds.

The bar was almost filled, but he felt sure he could elbow himself an opening.

Once he had a place at the bar, Clint signaled for the bartender and ordered a beer. When the man brought his drink, Clint crooked his finger to get the bartender to lean in.

"Is Mr. Town in?"

"He ain't come down yet," the bartender said.

"When he does, I'd like to see him."

The bartender shook his head.

"He don't see just anybody."

"He'll see me."

"Why?"

"My name's Clint Adams."

The bartender leaned away immediately and looked Clint up and down.

"That the truth?" he asked.

"As true as can be," Clint said. "Just tell him. Okay?"

"Sure, Mr. Adams," the bartender said. "Sure. I'll make sure he knows. Uh, where are you gonna be?"

"Right here, friend," Clint said, "drinking this beer."

"Naw," the bartender said, "not that beer." He snatched it cleanly from Clint's hand. "I'll getcha a better one."

Before he knew it, Clint had a colder beer in a cleaner glass in front of him.

"I'll tell the boss you're here, Mr. Adams," the bartender said.

Before Clint could say anything, the man was gone. He sipped the beer, found it excellent. He wondered what kind of swill everyone else was drinking.

Clint leaned against the bar, drinking his beer and watching the activity in the saloon. It seemed to be running with the precision of all the biggest and best gambling houses in the West. He wondered how well it would run when Lincoln Town was gone—because if he found out that Town had killed Juliet, that was what was going to happen.

The bartender returned, followed by a man who stopped every so often to glad-hand a customer. For this reason he made slow progress across the floor, giving Clint a chance to look him over.

He was tall, fit, appeared to be in his early forties or so. His hair was black, peppered with gray. He wore an expensive three-piece suit with an appropriately expensive watch fob dangling from the vest pocket.

He finished working his way across the room and headed directly for Clint.

"Mr. Adams?"

"That's right."

"Lincoln Town." He extended his hand for Clint to shake, which he did. "What brings the famous Gunsmith to our little town?"

"Actually, I'm here to visit a friend of mine. Maybe you know her? Juliet Fuller?"

"Oh," Town said, then, "oh God, this is awkward."

"What's awkward about it?" Clint asked. "You haven't married her, have you?"

"Married? No, no, that's not it," Town said, looking concerned. "Did you just arrive in town?"

"Yes," Clint said, "getting a cold beer was first on my list—after a hotel room, that is."

"Well, then . . . you don't know."

"Know what?"

"I'm sorry to have to tell you this, Mr. Adams," Town said, with what seemed like real regret, "but Juliet is . . . dead."

"Dead?" Clint feigned shock. "What happened?"

"She was strangled."

"You mean murdered?"

"Yes," Town said, "murdered."

"My God," Clint said, contriving to appear devastated.

"Would you like something stronger to drink?" Town asked. "On the house, of course."

"Yes," Clint said, "yes, I'll take a whiskey."

Town signaled to the bartender and had the man bring Clint a whiskey, which he downed.

"I'm so sorry to have to be the one to give you the bad news," Town said.

"Who killed her?"

"It's a mystery," Town said. "Nobody knows."

"But they're trying to find out, right?"

"I'm afraid the sheriff here isn't very experienced when it comes to murder."

"So nobody's doing anything?"

"I'm afraid not."

"How did you know Juliet?"

"She was only here for a short time," Town said, "but I'd like to think that we had become friends."

"*Friends?*"

"Oh, nothing like that," Town said. "*Just* friends."

"Did she have any other friends in town?"

"I'm sure she did," Town said.

"Then maybe her friends would be willing to hire somebody to find out who killed her."

"Hire somebody?" Town asked. "You mean like . . . a detective?"

"That's exactly what I mean," Clint said. "I happen to be friends with the finest private detective in the country. Talbot Roper, from Denver. Do you know him?"

"I know of him, of course, but . . . he doesn't come cheap."

"No, he doesn't."

"As I said," Town reiterated, "she was only here a short time . . ."

"What was her business?" Clint asked. "She sent me a telegram telling me she'd finally opened her own business, but she didn't tell me what it was." He knew that Town would only have to check a couple of places to find out that he was lying, but he didn't care. He wanted to see if the man would hang himself.

"Why don't we both have a drink," Town suggested, "and talk at my table?"

TEN

Clint didn't know if Lincoln Town was trying to get him drunk or not, but he kept having the bartender bring more drinks to the table. Every saloon owner Clint ever knew chose a table for themselves in their own establishment. It was usually a table that afforded a good view of the entire place.

"I would like it as much as you if someone could catch the killer," Town said.

"I doubt it," Clint said. "You didn't know her as well as I did."

"Okay, you're right," Town said. "I don't feel the loss the way you do. What can I do to help?"

"You're a businessman in this town," Clint said. "Was her business so good that someone would want to kill her to get it?"

Lincoln Town sat back in his chair and stared across the table at Clint.

"What is it?" Clint asked.

"You're barking up the wrong tree, there."

"How so?"

"As it happens, I now have Juliet's business," Town

said, "but I'm guessing you already knew that when you came in here."

Clint said, "You're right."

"Then what was this whole charade about?" Town demanded. "Free drinks?"

"I just wanted to meet you," Clint said, "see what you had to say for yourself."

"Somebody told you I killed her, didn't they?" Town asked. "Or had her killed?"

"It may have been mentioned."

"And you believed it?"

"Why not?" Clint asked. "I don't know you. That's why I came here, to get some idea of the kind of man you are."

"Well, you're not going to find that out in one afternoon, are you?" Town asked. "I tell you what. Come to work for me."

"What?"

"Work for me for a while," Town said. "That'll give you a good idea of the kind of man I am."

"Why don't I just talk to some of the people who work for you now?"

"That's not going to help you," Town said. "All you're going to get is their opinions. What you need are your own opinions."

"Well, forgive me for saying so," Clint said, "but I think I can form those without working for you."

He stood up.

"So what are your plans?" Town asked.

"I'm going to find out who killed Juliet," Clint said. "And when I do, God help them. No, I take that back. When I find them, God won't be able to help them.

"You'll kill them?" Town asked. "Why not let the law handle it?"

"Like they've handled it up to now?" Clint asked. "No, when it comes to Juliet's murder, I'm going to be the law, the judge, and the executioner."

"Why do I get the idea you're threatening me?"

"If you're feeling threatened," Clint said, "maybe it's because you're guilty of something."

"Even if I was guilty of something," Town responded, "threats from a two-bit gunman would not scare me."

Clint put his hands flat on the table and leaned forward.

"Better be careful, friend," he said. "I think a little of the real Lincoln Town might have just leaked out."

Town grinned tightly and said, "Adams, I don't think you want to meet the real Lincoln Town."

"Town," Clint replied, "I don't think you want to meet the real Gunsmith."

ELEVEN

Clint left the Pat Hand not sure what he had accomplished at all, except to alert Lincoln Town that he might be coming after him—perhaps not the smartest course of action to have taken.

He'd gone straight to the saloon from the whorehouse out of anger, without thinking things through. So the best course of action now was probably to take the time to think a bit. He could do that in his room, but after all the beer and whiskey he'd drunk with Town, he was starving. He stopped at the first café he saw, got a table away from the window, and ordered a steak. No harm thinking while tending to his stomach.

After Clint Adams left the saloon, Lincoln Town went to the bar and called the bartender over.

"What was that about, boss?" the man asked.

"None of your damned business," Town said. "Find Frank Cuddy and tell him I want him right away."

"Sure, boss."

"Do it now!"

"But, boss, the bar—"

"Move, or I'll fire your ass!"

"I'm goin'," the man said. He started around the bar, paused to take off his apron, then decided to leave it on because Town was glaring at him. As he ran out of the saloon, Town turned around and walked to his office.

Frank Cuddy was involved in a backroom poker game when the bartender found him.

"Get out, Artie," Cuddy said, before the man could speak.

"But Frank—"

"Out," Cuddy said, then to the other men at the table he said, "I raise."

"Frank, I can't go back without deliverin' the message," Artie wailed. "You know if the boss gets mad at me, he's gonna set you on me."

Cuddy grinned and said, "Yeah, you're right. Okay, deliver your message."

"He wants to see you right away."

"Okay," Cuddy said, "tell him I'll be there."

"Uh, when?"

"As soon as I'm done here."

Artie started to leave, then turned and asked, "With that hand, or the whole game?"

"Artie—"

"I'm goin'."

But when the bartender got to the door, he stopped, turned, and said, "It's got somethin' to do with Clint Adams."

Cuddy stopped what he was doing and turned around to look at the bartender for the first time.

"You sayin' the Gunsmith is in town?"

"That's right," Artie said. "He was in the saloon. I served him beer and whiskey while he talked to the boss."

"About what?"

"I dunno," Artie said. "He tol' me it's none of my business. Just tol' me to come and find you."

"You in or out, Frank?" one of the men asked.

"I'm out."

"But you raised—"

"I said I fold!"

Cuddy tossed his cards down on the table and then followed Artie out.

They had been playing five-card draw. One of the men turned Cuddy's cards over, revealing a full house.

"He's crazy," he said.

"Yeah," another man said, "but don't let him hear you say that. I guess I win this hand with two pair."

TWELVE

Clint was thinking that the best thing he might have done was accept the job offer from Lincoln Town without pushing the man. He might have been able to find out what he wanted to know from the inside. But it was too late for that. Town had been alerted that Clint wouldn't rest until he found Juliet's killer. He had two options. Get rid of the actual killer, or kill Clint.

He remembered the name one of the women had mentioned: Frank Cuddy. Perhaps the smart thing now would be to find out as much about this Cuddy as he could. That meant talking with the sheriff one more time. Who else would have information about a local gunny?

Clint finished his meal—which had been, at best, palatable—paid his bill and left the café. As he started walking in the direction of the sheriff's office, he saw the bartender from the Pat Hand hurrying along across the street, followed by another man. The two of them rushed into the Pat Hand without looking around. Clint was going to guess that Town had sent the bartender to fetch Cuddy, his hired gun.

It seemed obvious which way Lincoln Town was leaning.

When they entered the Pat Hand, Artie hurried around behind the bar while Cuddy walked across the room to Lincoln Town's office. He knocked and entered without waiting.

"You wanted to see me?" he asked.

Town regarded the man from behind his desk.

"Artie told you, didn't he?"

"Told me what?" Cuddy seated himself across from his boss. "Whataya talkin' about?"

"Come on, Frank," Town said. "When was the last time you came right over when I called for you? You always make me wait. Artie told you about Clint Adams, didn't he?"

"He might have mentioned the name."

"And I'll bet you even folded a winning hand to get your ass over here."

Cuddy grinned and said, "A full house. You're good, boss."

"Remember that," Town said.

"So what's the Gunsmith want in Silver Junction?"

"He was friends with Juliet Fuller."

"The whorehouse woman?"

"That's right."

"Does he know she's dead?"

"He didn't know when he arrived," Town said, "but he knows now."

"Did you tell him?"

"No," Town said, "he knew when he came in here. He must've gone to the house and talked to somebody."

"Who?"

"That's one of the things you're going to find out."

"And do what?"

"Just find out who told him," Town said, "and what they told him. We'll go from there."

"This is the Gunsmith, you know."

"I know it."

"This is my chance."

"Don't go off half-cocked, Frank," Town said. "You'll get your chance."

"Just make sure I do," Cuddy said.

Town leaned forward.

"Stay sway from Adams until I give you the word," he said. "You got that?"

"I got it."

"Yeah, but do you understand it?"

"I understand," Cuddy said irritably.

Town sat back.

"You're twenty-three years old, kid," he said. "You've got a lot of time ahead of you. Don't be in such an all-fired hurry all the time. Just relax."

"I am relaxed," Cuddy said. "I'm always relaxed."

"Good," Town said, "good. Get started, then. Go over to the house—and leave the girls alone."

"Tell the girls to leave me alone," Cuddy said, standing up. "They're all over me when I go in there."

"I'm sure they are."

Cuddy walked to the door, stopped with his hand on the knob.

"What does Adams look like?" he asked.

"Why do you want to know that?"

"How am I supposed to stay away from him if I don't know what he looks like?" the younger man asked.

Town stared at Cuddy for a few seconds, then laughed and said, "Nice try, Frank. Get out."

Cuddy left the office, walked directly to the bar, and called Artie over.

"Yeah?"

"What does Clint Adams look like?"

THIRTEEN

"Back so soon?" the sheriff asked.

"I couldn't stay away from your coffee."

"I've got to make a pot."

Clint held up his hand and said, "Actually, I'll pass. I just wanted to ask you a few more questions."

"About what?"

"Frank Cuddy."

"Whataya want to know about him?"

"How dependent is he on Lincoln Town?"

"Lemme see if I understand the question," Sheldon said. "You want to know if Cuddy will come after you himself, or if he'll wait for the word from Town."

"That's it."

Sheldon rubbed his jaw.

"That's a tough one," he said. "Cuddy's a hothead, but Town usually has him under control. But in your case . . . I don't know what to tell you."

"Okay," Clint said. "I just needed to find out whatever I could."

"You talk to Lincoln Town yet?"

"I did."

"And?"

"I messed it up," Clint said, shaking his head.

"You let him know you were comin' for him?"

"I'm afraid so."

"Well, he won't come," Sheriff Sheldon said. "He'll send Cuddy—but you already know that. That's why you're askin' about him."

"Right."

"How did Town react?"

"Well, first he offered me a job," Clint said. "Then he realized that I suspected him, and his . . . manner changed."

"If I was you," the sheriff said, "I'd warn whichever girl it was who told you about him."

"There was more than one," Clint said, "but I take your point."

"I gotta ask you, Adams . . ."

"Yeah?"

"Why not let it go?" Sheldon asked. "This is likely to be a big mess by the time you're finished. Was she worth it?"

"She was a friend of mine, Sheriff," Clint said. "Yeah, she was worth it."

Clint stepped out onto the boardwalk outside the sheriff's office and stopped. Before this was over, he was going to have to kill somebody. Was Juliet worth killing a man over? After all, he hadn't known her very long, just a few days, and that was a few years ago. But Clint had a way of holding on to his friends, and when someone took one away from him, it made him mad.

So his reply to the sheriff's question was the only one he could possibly have given. He was going to make a mess, he was going to have to kill someone—maybe more than one person—because his friend was worth it.

He turned and walked down the street until he was right across the street from the Pat Hand. He could hear the music and voices from inside. He didn't know if the man who had followed the bartender in had come out yet, but he was fairly certain that man was Frank Cuddy.

Since Clint didn't have much else to do, he decided to pick out a doorway and wait to see if the man came out. He wanted a better look.

Frank Cuddy had a drink amidst the din in the Pat Hand, but that didn't keep him from concentrating. Killing Clint Adams—the Gunsmith himself—was not only going to make him, it was going to allow him to leave Silver Junction, leave Lincoln Town, and go out on his own. It was something he'd been dreaming about since he was twelve and his parents had died.

From twelve to sixteen he was virtually a ward of the town. He ate someplace different every night, and he slept someplace different every night—and only after he did a day's work for somebody. He was fifteen when he discovered he had talent with a gun. It was while he was sweeping up at the gunsmith shop. No one was around so he loaded a gun, took it out back, and fired it six times. Damned if he didn't hit what he was pointing at all six times. He was a natural. But hitting his target wasn't everything. He started doing more and more work for Mr. Kyle—who was now dead and gone of natural causes—and began to practice not only with the gun, but with a gun belt. By the time he was sixteen he was ready to be emancipated—even though he didn't know what the word meant at the time.

From sixteen to twenty-one he plied his new trade, made his way with his gun, and the townspeople learned to fear him. Then, at twenty-one, he started working for

Lincoln Town. At first he was thrilled, even flattered, that such a man wanted him. Two years later he realized that he was doing all of Town's dirty work, while Town reaped the benefits. Well, that was okay, as long as Town continued to pay him well. Now, after two years, he had a nice poke put away. All he needed was the right circumstances to leave.

And finally, in the person of the Gunsmith, he had it. All he had to do was play it right. Town was right about one thing.

He needed to relax.

FOURTEEN

The man finally came out of the Pat Hand. From across the street he looked more like a boy with a gun than a man, but Clint knew that looks could be deceiving. Billy the Kid had proven that.

He didn't follow the young man. He didn't need to. All he'd wanted was a better look and now he'd gotten one. Now his next step was to go back to the whorehouse, which would no doubt be in full swing by this time of day. He needed to speak again with Louisa and Ginger, if just to warn them.

He knocked on the door and this time it was answered immediately by Regina in full makeup, a broad, welcoming smile on her face. She was wearing a tight gown that pushed her cleavage up almost under her chin.

When she saw him, though, she dropped the smile.

"Oh," she said, "it's you.

"May I come in?"

"It's business hours."

"That's all right," he said. "I won't take long. I just want to talk to Louisa and Ginger again."

"They're workin'," she said, putting her hands on her hips. "You'll have to pay for their time."

"Fine," he said. "Can I come in now?"

"Come ahead." She backed away to let him enter, then closed the door. "The girls are all in the drawing room— the ones who aren't upstairs, already. There are also some men in there, so don't spook anybody."

"I'll try not to."

He entered the room, saw a few men seated here and there with women pressed up against them, doing their best to sell themselves. They really didn't have to try that hard, though. Men in a whorehouse were pretty much already buying. It was just a matter of who.

He spotted Louisa in a corner, sitting on the arm of a chair in which a portly, sweating man sat. On his other side was a younger woman he was paying more attention to, a slender blonde who was probably about nineteen. As far as Clint was concerned, Louisa would have been the choice. More experience and more personality.

He walked over to the chair and heard the blonde telling the portly man, "I can really show you a good time," while rubbing his arm.

"Louisa," he said

She turned her head, looked over, and recognized Clint right away. She left the chair arm and came over to him. Her generous breasts were spilling out the top of her gown without benefit of being pushed up, as Regina's were.

"Did you find out who killed Juliet already?" she asked.

"No," he said, "but I need to talk with you."

"Well, I'm workin'—"

"I'll pay," he said.

"All right, then." She took his hand. "Come with me. I'll have to tell Regina."

"She's the boss, huh?"

"Until Mr. Town gets around to actually making some-one the mad—uh, the hostess."

They found Regina, and Louisa told her she was going upstairs with Clint.

"Make sure you get paid first," was all Regina said.

Louisa smiled, pulled Clint along by the hand, and said, "Come on, honey."

He followed her up the stairs, watching how her chunky buttocks played beneath the fabric of her gown.

She led him down a hall past some rooms that were ob-viously occupied, judging from the sounds coming from within. Her room was all the way at the end of the hall. She opened the door, tugged him inside, and then closed the door behind them. Immediately, she began to disrobe.

"Whoa, wait a minute," he said. "I just came to talk."

"I told you that Juliet told me all about you," she said. "I want to see if it's true."

She dropped her gown to the floor and stood before him completely naked. She was older than the other girls, but she was lovely. Her breasts were large, with heavy, rounded undersides and large brown nipples. Her waist was probably thicker than when she had been a girl, her hips broader, and her buttocks wider, but the whole pic-ture was one that appealed to him—a lot, judging from the way his own body was responding. To not only the sight of her, but the smell, as well.

She looked down at his crotch and smiled lasciviously.

"I can see you're not totally disinterested."

"I'm not disinterested at all, Louisa," he said, "but I have a rule—"

"I know," she said, coming closer to him. "You don't pay. That's okay. I don't care."

"What will you tell Regina?"

"I'll say we talked, and I forgot to take your money."

"You'll get in trouble."

"I don't care."

She put her arms around his neck, pressed her breasts against him, and kissed him hungrily.

He was lost.

FIFTEEN

Clint moved in closer so he could cup those big breasts in his hands.

"Do we talk while we're doing this?" he asked.

"On, no," she said, undoing his gun belt, "this first, then we talk. I want your full attention."

She took the gun belt and was about to toss it aside when he stopped her and said, "Uh-uh. It's got to be in reach."

"I know," she said. "I was gonna hang it on the bedpost because that's where we're gonna end up."

"Okay, then."

He watched as she walked across the room and hung the belt on the post. Then she turned to face him, cupping her own breasts, thumbing her own hardening nipples.

"Come here," she said. As he did, she held her breasts up to him. He bent his head and licked the nipples, then sucked and bit them. She released her breasts and held his head there while he enjoyed her nipples.

Finally, he stepped away from her and took off his own clothes, which seemed to be suffocating him. When he removed his last garment, his erection sprang into view and she caught her breath and then smiled.

"Well," she said, happily clapping her hands together once, "Juliet was right about that!"

She got on her knees in front of him and lovingly cradled his testicles in her hands while her mouth swooped down on his cock. She took him inside and suckled him wetly, bobbing her head up and down while continuing to fondle him. He felt his legs getting weak, so he bent his knees a little and put his hands on her head. His intention was to try to extract himself from her hot mouth, but in the end he just couldn't do it. It felt too damn good! Before long he was exploding into her mouth, and she continued to suck him until he was dry. When he was done, she released him, but continued to fondle him, lick him, and suck him until he was hard again.

"And she was right about that, too," she said.

She stood up and, still holding him by the penis, pulled him to the bed. She lay down on her back, and he climbed on the bed with her, began to kiss her neck and shoulder, her breasts and nipples, her belly, and worked his way down to her pussy, which he assumed was what she wanted. If this was a test, he was determined to pass.

He began to lick her wet pussy, up and down with long tongue strokes, and when he got to the top, he'd poke her clit with the tip of his tongue. When he licked his way back down, he'd poke her again, this time entering her with his tongue. With each poke her hips jumped and she gasped. Finally, he inserted his middle finger into her pussy while concentrating on her clit with his tongue. He circled it and circled it, and then flicked it with the tip of his tongue, back and forth, up and down, over and over again until he felt it grow hard. Finally, as he continued to fuck her with his finger and tongue, she suddenly gasped, grew rigid, and then gushed all over his mouth.

"Oh my God!" she cried out. "Jesus." She reached down and pushed his face away from her. "I've never done that before!"

"Never?" he asked, getting to his knees.

"God," she said, and he could see that her legs were shaking. "I've been with a lot of men in my time, and no one's ever made me do that. That was . . . scary!"

"Scary bad?"

"Scary good, you beautiful man," she said. "I guess Juliet was right about everything, but just to make sure . . . get up here and fuck me good!"

"Yes, ma'am."

He straddled her, pressed the tip of his hard penis against her, and then slid into her. He went in to the hilt, stayed there a moment while he kissed her, and drew out before plunging in again. He began to take her in long slow strokes, and then went increasingly faster. She began to gasp and clutch at him, wrapping her legs around him so that he could feel her strong thighs tightening on him. He slid his hands beneath them so he could cup her big butt and pull her toward him when he fucked her.

They fucked that way for a while, and if Regina had been standing outside the door listening to be sure of what they were doing, there would be no doubt. They were both loud about it, and the bed was jumping up and down, making a hell of a racket.

When he withdrew from her, she protested until he flipped her over onto her belly. Then she got the idea and hiked her butt up in the air for him. He didn't know if she wanted him to put it in her ass or not, but instead he just edged up between those big thighs and slid right back into her pussy. He began fucking her that way, so hard that they made slapping sounds when his belly met her buttocks. She began to push back against him whenever he entered her and, finally, her insides seemed to wrap around his cock and pull his orgasm from him. Every spurt into her was so good it was pleasure and pain at the same time. She started to say, "Oooh, ooh, ooh," as he filled her, sounding more like an animal than a woman. When he was finally done, he withdrew, and the two last spurts from his penis landed on her butt.

He stayed on his knees behind her and gasped, "Now can we talk?"

She looked at him over her shoulder, but she was breathing too hard to speak, so she simply rolled her eyes and nodded her head.

SIXTEEN

They lay side by side while they talked, still catching their breath.

"Lincoln Town won't kill me," she told him, "or any of the other girls."

"He won't? How can you be so sure?"

"Because whatever else he is, he's a good business-man. Killing one of his girls wouldn't be smart."

"But you're not his girls," Clint pointed out. "You're Juliet's girls."

"As far as he's concerned, we're his."

"And why do you put up with that?"

"Because we need to make a living, Clint," she said. "You can't fault the girls for staying here. They all need the money."

"Including you?"

"Yeah, including me. I could've been loyal to Juliet's memory and left, but I don't have anyplace to go."

"I'm not judging you, Louisa," he said.

"You better not," she said, taking his hand and placing it on the black bush between her legs, "Or you get no more of this."

He slid his finger along her slit and right into her and she jumped and yelped.

"Oooh, oh," she sad, "I'm still too sore . . ."

He removed his finger and said, "Sorry. I didn't mean to hurt you."

"Never mind," she said, "it hurt so good."

He stood up and started to get dressed.

"Louisa, what do you think would happen if I took this place over? Would the girls stay?"

"They'd stay and love it," she said. "You mean to do that? Take this place away from Town?"

"It's one way for me to go," he said. "That would tweak him as a businessman."

"He'd send Cuddy after you for sure," Louisa said. "That boy is a born killer."

"Well, I'm going to have to face Cuddy sooner or later," Clint said, strapping on his gun. "No point in dwelling on it. It's going to happen."

"Will you kill him?"

"Before he can kill me," he said, "if I can."

"No," she said, "I meant, can you kill him? Outdraw him?"

He stopped a moment, then said, "I don't know, Louisa. I've never seen the boy draw his gun. I guess maybe we'll all find that out at the same time."

He walked to the bed and kissed her.

"I'm gonna stay here and rest awhile," she said. "You tell Regina you wore me out as you go out, huh? Lay it on thick?"

He laughed and said, "Sure, I can do that."

"I gotta say, Clint Adams," she commented as he went to the door, "Juliet sure didn't lie about you at all."

"Nice to know I passed inspection," he said.

"With flying colors!" she shouted as he went out.

When he got downstairs, he found himself immediately confronted by Regina.

"Where's Louisa?" she demanded.

"She decided to get some rest," Clint said. "Seems I wore her out."

"Is she all right?" Regina demanded. "You know, if you hurt any of the girls—"

"She's not hurt, Regina," he said. "She's fine. Is Ginger available?"

"You just finished with Louisa and you want Ginger?" she asked.

"What can I say?" he asked, spreading his hands. "My appetites are insatiable."

She frowned, and he doubted she knew what the word meant, and was equally sure she'd die before asking.

"She's in the drawing room."

"Thanks." He left before she could ask if he had paid.

When he entered the room, he saw it was much the same as before. People—different people—were in the same positions. Off in one corner Ginger sat next to a meek-looking man, who seemed very jumpy. She was talking to him and rubbing his thigh.

He approached and said, "Ginger?"

When Ginger saw Clint, she immediately abandoned the meek man and rushed to his side.

"I heard you were back."

"Just to talk."

She pouted. "I heard you went upstairs with Louisa."

"Again," he said, "just to talk." At least, that had been his intention. "Can we go to your room?"

"Just to talk?" she asked.

"Just for a few minutes."

"Sure," she said, with a shrug, "why not?"

She took his hand and tugged him toward the stairs.

SEVENTEEN

As soon as they entered her room, she turned, pinned him to the door, and kissed him, thrusting her tongue into his mouth.

"Ginger—"

She wouldn't let him talk, kept kissing him, reaching between them to massage his crotch.

Finally he pulled free of her mouth and said, "Wait, wait!"

"If you want me to answer your questions," she said breathily, "you're gonna have to pay my price."

"Ginger," he said, "I just finished paying Louisa's price—"

"She got to you before me?" Ginger demanded. "Damn it! We had a bet."

"Well, you lost the bet, so let's talk," he said, holding her at arm's length.

"Oh, no," she said, "you don't get off that easy." She sniffed. "You're right, I can smell Louisa on you."

"See? I haven't even had time for a bath—"

"Don't worry about it," she said. "Louisa and I have

worked together before. She actually tastes good, don't
you think?

"Well, yeah—"

"So do I," she said. She stepped back and pulled her
dress off over her head. She was long and lean, with
small breasts and lovely pink nipples. The hair between
her legs was like fire, as red as the hair on her head. And
she had freckles, like most redheads, almost everywhere.

"Ginger," he said, "I don't think I can—"

She stepped closer to him and cupped his crotch, finding him hard.

"I don't think you'll have a problem," she said, tug-
ging him towards the bed by his gun belt.

She removed his gun belt and hung it on the bedpost,
then undid his trousers and pulled them down. Sure
enough, his penis was as hard as it had been during the
time he had been with Louisa. Even he was surprised.

"It's your own fault, you know," she said, taking him in
her hands. "Juliet talked about you . . . a lot. It made me
and Louisa very envious and curious. You can't blame us
for wanting to find out for ourselves."

"I suppose not . . ."

She pulled off his boots so he could kick his trousers
away, then took him deep into her mouth and moaned. He
wondered if he was going to have the strength to walk out
of there . . .

Later his head was between her legs and he was delving
into that fiery patch with his tongue. He found her wet
and salty, very hot and sensitive. She began to shudder almost immediately and even while riding the crest of one
orgasm implored him not to stop. He had no intention of
stopping. Once she had gotten him going, he wanted their

coupling as much as she did. At one point he had flipped her over as he'd done with Louisa, but instead of lying flat and hiking her butt, Ginger got to her knees and held onto the bedpost while he pounded her from behind.

Now he continued to lick her, bringing her to completion again and again until she pushed him away—but instead of stopping she grabbed him, pulled him on top of her, and begged him to fuck her again. She was as hungry for it as Louisa had been, but the fact that she was about ten years younger kept her going longer. He only hoped he could keep up with her, considering how much energy he had expended with Louisa.

He recalled what Ginger said about having worked with Louisa before. It occurred to him that it might have been better for him if he'd "talked" to them together . . .

Ginger said the same thing Louisa said about Lincoln Town.

"He'd never kill me," she said. "I'm a big money-maker here. He's too good a businessman."

"Well," he said, "I just felt the need to warn the two of you."

"The only way we'd get killed is if he loses control of Cuddy," she said. "He's crazy, and might do it on his own."

"Why not leave, then?"

Again, her answer echoed Louisa's.

"I have no place to go," she said, then added, "and even if I did, I have no money."

"Then maybe you better start saving some," he told her.

She sat up in bed and pulled up her knees, so that her pink nipples were just barely touching her thighs.

"You wanna pay my way, or Louisa's way, out of here, be my guest."

"I'll keep it in mind" he said. He slid around to get out of bed, but she was on his back before he could, wrapping her arms around him.

"Not yet," she said. "I don't want to go back downstairs yet."

"But I—"

"Your own fault, again," she told him, tonguing his ear. "After being with you, I can't be with some sloppy cowpoke or some fat farmer." She bit his earlobe, licked his neck, and looked down at his crotch, where his penis was swelling again.

"Look," she said, "you don't really want to leave, either."

Clint looked down at his own body with wonder. It couldn't be him, he thought, it had to be these women. They were really good at what they did.

"No," he said, "I guess I don't."

EIGHTEEN

Clint managed to leave the whorehouse without running into Regina again. He did this by creeping down the stairs, waiting for Regina to leave the entry hall of the big house, and then sneaking out the front door.

He walked back to his hotel on shaky legs. Louisa and Ginger had been warned about Lincoln Town, and both women had satisfied their curiosity about Clint Adams. Everybody was happy, right? Everybody but Juliet Fuller. She was still dead.

And Clint Adams wasn't happy. As he reached the hotel, he realized he didn't even know where Juliet was buried. He veered away and continued on until he found the undertaker. Rather than go back to the sheriff with his question, he decided to ask this man.

He entered the funeral parlor and a bell hanging from the ceiling rang, alerting the undertaker to his presence. When the man appeared, Clint was surprised. He looked more like a gambler than an undertaker and he was young for the job.

"Can I help you, friend?"

He was also wearing a gun on his hip.

"Are you the undertaker?" Clint asked.

"I'm wearin' the black suit, ain't I?" the man said with a smile. Clint put his age at about twenty-five. "Don't let the gun fool you. I used to be a gunfighter. I put a lot of men into the ground with my gun. Now I'm doin' it a different way. The name's Giles, Baron Giles."

"Clint Adams," Clint said, accepting the man's outstretched hand.

"Whoa," Giles said, releasing Clint's hand and backing up. "Look who I'm braggin' to."

"No problem," Clint said. "You want to brag, be my guest."

Giles was looking Clint up and down. Clint hoped the man would not decide at that moment to go back to being a gunfighter.

"What can I do for you, Mr. Adams?" he asked.

"I just got to town and was looking for a friend of mine, Juliet Fuller."

"Oh. You found out she's dead?"

"That's right," Clint said.

"I can't help you with that," Giles said. "I don't know who killed her. Nobody does."

"I'm interested in where she's buried," Clint said. "You handled that, didn't you?"

"Yep, I did," Giles said. "Put her in one of my best boxes. Damn shame. She was a nice lady."

"You knew her?"

"A little bit."

"Professionally?"

"Her profession or mine?"

"Either one."

"No."

If the answer was no, Clint wondered why the man needed the question clarified.

"Where is she buried?"

"We got a little boot hill on the outskirts of town," Baron Giles told him.

"Can I walk or do I need to saddle my horse?"

"You could walk, but I got a buggy out back. I can take you up there."

"I can get my horse—"

"It's no trouble," Giles said. "Call it professional courtesy."

Clint didn't bother telling Giles that he didn't consider his profession to be "gunfighter."

"Okay," he said, "thanks."

Standing in front of Juliet's grave, Clint felt for the first time that she was really dead. The marker simply read JULIET FULLER.

"Nobody knew how old she was," Giles explained.

Clint just nodded.

"Were you two, uh, close?" Giles asked.

"We were friends."

"Gonna stick around to find out who killed her?"

"Oh, yes," Clint said.

"Think you'll need any help?"

Clint turned his head and looked at the younger man. In his experience, men who proclaimed themselves to be gunfighters were rarely more than men who wanted to be gunfighters.

"I might."

Giles spread his hands and said, "I'm available."

"You any good with that iron?" Clint asked.

Giles drew and fired twice. Clint liked his move, looked to see if he'd shot what he'd fired at. There was a grave marker about twenty feet away for a man named Mooney. There were now two bullet holes, one in each letter O.

Or had they been there before?

NINETEEN

Clint told Giles that now that he knew how far it was to town he preferred to walk.

"You'll come and see me if you need help," Giles said.

"I'll think about it."

"Fair enough."

Walking back, Clint thought about those two holes in the grave marker. Even if Baron Giles had put them there, it didn't mean he'd ever faced a man with his gun. Also, Clint didn't like the fact that the man had not ejected his spent loads and replaced them with live ones after his demonstration. Any man who had made his way with a gun would instantly reload.

He decided that Giles was a man who could hit what he shot at, who might have the ability to be a gunfighter—as he claimed—but had no experience. And a man with no experience was not someone who could be relied on. Not until he actually had some experience under his belt.

So, if Clint needed help, Baron Giles was on the list, but down toward the bottom.

Still, there was no harm checking the man out with the

sheriff, but he decided to do that in the morning. He didn't want to bother the lawman again that day.

Frank Cuddy entered the whorehouse and grabbed Regina by the arm, pulling her through a curtained doorway into a small office off the entry hall.

"Ow, Frank, you're hurtin' me!" she complained.

"That ain't all I'm gonna do," Cuddy said, "if you don't answer my questions."

"Frank," she said, "you know I answer all your questions. You don't have to hurt me."

He released her arm, but said with a smile, "Yeah, but ain't it more fun this way?"

She wanted to say no, but didn't dare.

"Clint Adams was here," Cuddy said. "*Linc* wants to know who he talked to."

She also knew that Cuddy would never call Lincoln Town *Linc* to his face.

"Clint Adams?"

"You know, that friend of Juliet's."

"Oh, him," she said. "Yeah, he was here."

"Well," he said, after a few seconds, "who was he with? Who did he talk to?"

"He went upstairs with Louisa," she said, "and then he went upstairs with Ginger."

"Where is he now?"

"I don't know," she said. "He might still be with Ginger. I didn't see him leave."

"Go upstairs and find out," Cuddy said. "Where's Louisa?"

"She's in the drawing room with the other girls."

"Send her in here before you go up."

"Okay."

"And don't tell them nothin'!" he warned, as she was going out.

"I ain't got nothin' to tell them even if I wanted to," she answered, and got out fast.

Regina found Ginger alone in her room, sitting on the bed with her dress on.

"Where's that Adams fella?" she asked.

"He left," Ginger said. "We finished."

"Where's the money?"

"Damn!" Ginger said.

"You forgot?"

"I sure did," Ginger said. "He fucked my brains out."

"Well, you better find 'em again," Regina said. "Cuddy's downstairs and he wants to see you."

"That bastard?"

"Say that to his face," Regina challenged.

"I will."

"You'll have to wait your turn," Regina said. "He's with Louisa right now. She also forgot to get paid."

"Cuddy better not hurt her."

"What would you do about it?"

"We're not all as desperate for this job as you are, Regina," Ginger said.

"Yeah," Regina said, "you are."

"Oh, we're desperate, all right, honey," Ginger said, standing up. "We're just not as desperate as you are."

TWENTY

As Louisa entered the small office, Cuddy reached for her arm. She pulled away.

"Don't try that with me, you little bastard," she said. "I'll slap you silly."

"That's big talk for an old whore," Cuddy said, chuckling.

"What do you want, Cuddy?" she asked. "We're busy here tonight."

"Linc wants to know what you said to Clint Adams," Cuddy told her.

"What do you think I said?" she asked. "I told him that Mr. Town had Juliet killed . . . probably by you. If I was you, I'd leave town as soon as possible before the Gunsmith comes looking for you.'"

"I don't need advice from an old whore."

"That the biggest insult you can think to throw at me?" she asked. "Fact of the matter is, I *am* an old whore. Are we done?"

"Depends. Is that what you really told Adams?"

She put her hands on her hips and said, "That's what I really told him."

He walked up to her and slapped her across the face. She reacted instantly and slapped him back—harder.

"That all you got, boy?"

They faced each other, each sporting a red hand mark on their cheeks, as Ginger pushed the curtain aside and walked in.

"Are you two finished?" she asked. "Why don't you just have sex, already?"

"I wouldn't stick my dick in this shriveled up old . . ." he started, then just let it trail off. "Get out, you old bitch.

Louisa turned and winked at Ginger on her way out.

"You wanted to see me?" Ginger asked the younger man.

"You ain't as stupid as that old cow, Ginger," Cuddy said.

"Thanks . . . I think."

"You wanna go upstairs?" he asked.

She sighed and said, "I ain't got time for a free poke, Cuddy. What do you want?"

"Linc wants to know what you said to Clint Adams."

"What did Louisa say?"

"She said she told him Linc killed that bitch you used to work for," he answered.

"That he killed her?" Ginger asked. "Or you did?"

He narrowed his eyes and asked, "Then you told him the same thing?"

"Pretty much."

"Then you are as stupid as that cow."

"I guess I am. Are we done?"

"What makes you think I won't kill you, too? And her?" Cuddy asked.

"You would," Ginger said, "if he told you to . . . but he won't."

"What makes you so sure?"

"Because he's a businessman, and a good one," she said. "He wouldn't want you killin' his inventory."

"Don't be so sure," he said.

"Is that all?"

"Yeah," Cuddy said, with disgust, "that's all, get out."

As Ginger left, Cuddy put his hand to his cheek, which was still stinging. That old whore packed a wallop.

In the drawing room Ginger went over to where Louisa was sitting.

"What were you thinking, slapping him like that?" she asked. "He's gonna kill you for sure."

"I don't care," she said. "I'm not going to let that little pissant walk all over me."

"Well, he may end up walking all over your body."

"Clint will kill him," Louisa said. "As soon as he's sure it was him who killed Juliet, he'll kill him—and Lincoln Town."

"I hope you're right," Ginger said. "Clint is just one man."

"Maybe," Louisa said, "but what a man."

Both women exchanged a glance, and then each had the good grace to blush.

Cuddy left, steaming. He liked Ginger, but that old whore Louisa was asking for it. How dare she slap him like that? There was no way he would've let her know how much it hurt. He almost drew his gun and shot her on the spot, but he couldn't go against Lincoln Town by killing one of his girls.

At least, not yet.

TWENTY-ONE

The next morning Clint went in search of a decent breakfast. Eventually, he found a small restaurant that was doing a brisk business. He figured the town couldn't be that wrong so he went inside.

As he entered, he saw that the place was so crowded there were no tables, but that problem was soon solved when Sheriff Walt Sheldon waved at him from a table in the back.

"Come and join me," Sheldon said, as Clint reached his table. "You picked the right place for breakfast. Best in town."

"Thanks," Clint said.

A waiter came over and poured Clint a cup of coffee, took his order of steak and eggs.

Clint tried the coffee and nodded approvingly.

"How did your day end up yesterday?" Sheldon asked.

"It ended quietly," Clint said.

"Did you talk to those ladies about Lincoln Town?"

"I warned them, if that's what you mean."

"And?"

"Neither of them seemed particularly concerned," Clint said, and explained to the lawman their reasoning.

"They might be right," the sheriff said, when Clint was done. "I mean, they are right about him being a good businessman. I don't know if they're right about him being responsible for Miss Fuller's murder."

"That's for me to find out," Clint said. "I'm glad I ran into you this morning, though."

"Why's that? Aside from giving you a place to sit?" Sheldon asked.

"I met your undertaker yesterday."

Sheldon smiled. "Giles? Fancies himself a gunman. Must've been thrilled to meet you."

"Does he have any experience?"

"As an undertaker? Or a gunman?"

"Well, he buried Juliet, so I guess that gives him experience as an undertaker. What about with his gun? And where's he from?"

"He's local," Sheldon said. "Grew up here. His father was the undertaker for years. As for experience, he's won some sharpshooting contests."

"That's it? Has he ever faced anybody?"

"He's never shot at anything that was alive," the sheriff said. "And that includes animals. Only targets, standing objects, like that."

"Oh."

The waiter appeared with Clint's plate and set it down in front of him. The smell made his stomach growl. He cut into the steak, took some egg, and sampled a mouthful of the food.

"How is it?" Sheldon asked.

Clint nodded. He'd had better, but the sheriff had not promised that it would be good, only that it was the best food in town.

"It's fine," he said, after he washed it down with a swallow of coffee.

"So don't tell me," the sheriff said, "let me guess. He wants to help the famous Gunsmith?"

"He offered me his gun, yes," Clint said.

"And what did you say?"

"I said I'd think about it."

"I guess no one will ever know about him until he gets a chance," Sheldon said. "Right now he's an undertaker who'd rather be a gunfighter."

"He sort of put it the other way around to me," Clint said. "Insinuated that he had put his gun down to be an undertaker."

"Well, everyone in town knows what he really is," Sheldon said. "He only tries those stories on strangers. But you don't anticipate needing help, do you? Against Town and Cuddy?"

"I guess that depends."

"On what?"

"On whether or not they think they'll need help."

Clint and the sheriff chatted about the town, which the sheriff said was really starting to show some growth.

"Might even have another whorehouse soon," he added.

"And how would Mr. Town feel about that?"

"Not good," the sheriff said. "In fact, from what I hear, we may be getting a big gambling house, saloon, and whorehouse all in one."

"Who's bringing something like that into town?" Clint asked.

"A gambler," Sheldon said, "that's all I know."

"Well," Clint said, "I guess I'll have to see what I can do to help the newcomer have a clear field."

TWENTY-TWO

Clint insisted on paying for breakfast—"After all, you shared your table with me"—and then the two men left the restaurant and stopped on the boardwalk out front.

"What's next for you?" Sheldon asked.

"Asking questions," Clint said. "A lot of them."

"Are you expecting to find something out?" Sheldon asked. "Or just push until somebody pushes back?"

"Both, I suppose," Clint said. "They might both work. We'll just have to wait and see."

"I have to get to work," Sheldon said. "Just . . . keep me informed, will you?"

"Sure, Sheriff. Aren't you going to tell me not to shoot anyone while I'm in your town?"

"Would it do any good?"

"Probably not."

The sheriff waved his hand. "Then why waste my breath? Have a good day."

The sheriff went one way and Clint stepped off the walk and went another.

* * *

Lincoln Town sat behind his desk, considering his options. Outside, in the saloon, he could hear someone—probably Artie—sweeping up, taking chairs down off the tables, getting the place ready for the day's business.

When Cuddy returned the evening before, Town had seen the red hand mark on his cheek, but hadn't mentioned it. He knew it would have been Louisa who did that. Then, when Cuddy told him what Louisa and Ginger had to say, Town had dismissed him. Now he had to decide what to do. Those two whores were way too free with their mouths. That was bad, especially with Clint Adams in town.

Should he take care of them first? Or the Gunsmith first?

Cuddy woke that morning alone in his cabin. It was really a small, one-room shack that someone had abandoned years ago and he'd moved into. It was cold in the winter and hot in the summer, but at this time of year it was perfect. It didn't matter that there were spaces between the boards that made up the walls, letting the light in. He didn't sleep that well, anyway.

He got to his feet and put on yesterday's clothes, grabbed his gun belt, and strapped it on. He drew his gun several times to make sure it didn't stick. Never knew when he was going to need it, especially with the Gunsmith in town.

He checked his pocket, found a few coins there. It was breakfast at the Pat Hand, again. He knew Artie would feed him, if only because the man was afraid of him.

He left his shack, hoping that Lincoln Town would have his mind made up today. Cuddy could still feel the sting of Louisa's hand on his face. Kill her, kill Adams, he wanted Town to tell him. He preferred to do the woman first, because that was sure to bring Clint Adams after him. Then when he killed the Gunsmith, it would be a clear case of self-defense.

Clint went to the office of the local paper, the *Silver Junction Journal,* and arranged to read the copies that came out immediately following the murder. What he read made him angry. There was no call for a quick solution. In fact, Juliet Fuller's murder was treated like it was the killing of just another whore.

"I don't get this," he said to the editor, a man with greased black hair and a nameplate identifying him as Arthur Dent.

"Don't get what?"

"This story of Juliet Fuller's murder," Clint said. "There's not much here. Don't you care if her killer's caught? Doesn't the town care?"

The man looked at Clint as if he were a schoolteacher and Clint a difficult child.

"She wasn't from here," he said.

"So?"

"She had just come to town the month before," Dent said. "Nobody had much of an investment in her."

"Investment?"

"This is a close-knit community, mister," Dent said. "She wasn't part of the community. Maybe, if she'd lived here longer, she would have become part of it, but when she died, she wasn't." The man shrugged, as if that explained it all.

Clint knew there was no point pursuing it, so he gave the man back his newspaper and left. Outside he resolved that by the time this was all over, the town of Silver Junction was going to remember Juliet Fuller.

TWENTY-THREE

Baron Giles knew Clint Adams was never going to come to him for help. He knew that the man saw right through his malarkey. What he was going to have to do was prove himself. He knew he could hit anything he shot at. It was just like pointing his finger. He'd proven that time and again in sharpshooting contests—especially with a handgun.

And he knew he had a fast draw. What he didn't know was how he would react in a situation where someone was shooting back at him.

He'd spent years helping his father in his undertaker business and had taken it over when the old man died. His mother was already gone by then, and he had no brothers or sisters. He had to keep the business going so he could eat, but what he really wanted to do was hit the trail and make his way with his gun.

He might be able to do that, once he had proven himself to Clint Adams.

And to himself.

* * *

After breakfast Frank Cuddy went to the office and knocked on the door. Lincoln Town shouted for him to come in.

"You're early," Town said.

"I had breakfast outside," Cuddy said, jerking his thumb toward the saloon.

"Why doesn't that surprise me?" Town had a half-finished cup of coffee on his desk. Cuddy sat opposite him.

"What are we doin' today?" he asked. He was anxious and not covering it well.

"I haven't decided yet," Town said. "I might bring in some more help."

"Like who?"

"I don't know," Town said. "I might leave that up to you."

Cuddy shifted in his seat and said, "I don't need no help, but I can think of a couple of boys I could bring in."

"Okay," Town said, "come up with a couple of names and let 'em know."

"What about those bitches?"

"I've got to see if I can replace those bitches before I decide to get rid of them."

"You afraid to kill them?"

"It's just good business, Cuddy," Town said. "I don't do anything that isn't good business. Remember that."

"I don't have to," Cuddy said. "You're the business-man. I do all my business with this." He touched his gun.

"You're going to have to start using your head more if you want to get anywhere in life, Frank."

Cuddy didn't like the "use your head" lecture. For one thing he thought he was smart enough to get by. He wasn't the hothead everyone thought he was. If he was, Clint Adams would be dead by now and he'd be on his way. But Town had been good to him, and he had some loyalty to the man, so he wasn't going to pull the trigger on Clint Adams until the man said so.

Unless he took too damn long to do it.

Clint spent the morning asking questions, mostly of people who either lived or worked in the vicinity of the whorehouse. Men answered his questions readily. Some asked, with worried expressions, if the whorehouse was going to close. He told them he didn't think so. Women didn't want to talk about the whorehouse, but they, too, asked if the place was going to close. He gave them the same reply.

By noon he was done talking. Nobody had seen anything the night Juliet Fuller was killed, or if they had, they weren't saying.

He stopped into the same restaurant where he'd had breakfast, just to have a cup of coffee and consider his next move. This time it was Clint who spotted someone when they came in. There were plenty of tables available, but he waved that person over, anyway.

"Good morning," Louisa said, sitting down across from him.

"It's afternoon."

"Not for me," she said.

He called the waiter over.

"Is that all you're having?" she asked, indicating his coffee.

"Yes."

"Have a piece of pie with me," she said. "I like to have pie for breakfast."

They ordered an apple pie for her, and a peach pie for him.

"What have you been up to today?" she asked.

"Asking questions."

"Get any answers?"

"No."

"Who have you been talking to?"

"Your neighbors."

"You're not going to get anything from them," she said, "especially not the married ones."

"I found that out," he said. "The men are afraid you're going to close down, and the women are afraid you won't."

"I'm surprised the women haven't gotten together and burned us out."

The waiter brought their pie and a fresh pot of coffee, then poured a cup for Louisa. He seemed nervous around Louisa, and Clint assumed he was a past customer of hers.

"Thank you, Carl," she said to him.

"Louisa, what have you heard about another place coming into town?"

"Place? What kind of place?"

"Gambling, a saloon, and a whorehouse." Clint replied.

"I haven't heard anything," she said, "but why would I? Why would any of us? We're just whores."

"Come on," Clint said, "you hear as much or more than a bartender does. Pillow talk is even more reliable than bar talk."

"Drunk or having sex is about the same, huh?" she asked.

"Drunk and having sex is even better," he said. "Really loosens men's tongues."

"Well," she said, "in this case I can't help you. I haven't heard a thing, but I'll ask some of the other girls."

People were starting to come in for lunch, but two

couples saw Louisa and the women pulled the men out. Others stayed, but the women gave her disapproving looks and admonished their men not to look. Louisa sighed.

"I'd better finish my pie and get out. I'm bad for business."

"Let them leave if they don't like it."

"I can't blame them," she said. "Their husbands are getting something from me they're not getting at home."

"Well, maybe if they gave it to their husbands at home, they wouldn't have to come to you."

"Well, now," she said, "that would be good for them, but not for me."

They both finished their coffee and pie and he walked out with her, admiring the way she kept her head high and didn't look at anyone.

Outside, she said, "More questions for you?"

"I don't know who to ask," he said.

"Then what are you going to do?"

"I'll figure something out."

"Well, be careful," she said. "I might have lit a fire under Cuddy yesterday."

"What did you do?"

"I slapped him in the face."

"And he took that?"

"Well, he slapped me first," she said, "but I couldn't let the little pissant get away with it."

"I'll pay him back for that," Clint promised.

She touched his face and said, "I know you will, and you'll get justice for poor Juliet."

"I'm sure going to try."

"Come and see me," she said, "or Ginger. No charge, and we're not competitive."

"I'll remember."

She smiled and walked away. He watched her for one block, then stepped off the boardwalk and crossed the street.

Frank Cuddy watched Louisa walk away from Clint Adams, and then watched Adams cross over. He'd spotted Louisa when he came out of the Pat Hand and followed her. After a peek through the window to see who she was meeting, he retreated across the street to wait. He waited for Adams to be out of the way, then fell into step behind Louisa.

TWENTY-FOUR

Clint was in a saloon called the Branch House when Sheriff Sheldon came in, spotted him, and joined him at the bar. It was just after three, and Clint had come in for a beer to wet his throat, which was dry from talking to people all afternoon.

"Sheriff, can I buy you a beer?"

"I don't think so," the lawman said. "I think you'd better come with me."

"What's going on?" Clint asked. "Am I under arrest?"

"Nothin' like that," Sheldon said. "Just come along."

Clint had one more swallow of beer and then followed the sheriff outside.

"What's going on, Sheriff?"

"I've got some bad news for you."

"What?"

"There's been another killing."

"What? Who?"

"Another one of the women from the whorehouse."

"Jesus. Who?"

"Her name's Louisa."

Clint stopped in his tracks.

"What?"

The sheriff stopped.

"You knew her?"

"I saw her earlier today," Clint said.

"Where?

"In that restaurant where you and I had breakfast," Clint said. "We had a cup of coffee together."

"Did she say where she was goin' after she left you?" the lawman asked.

"Back to the house."

They started walking again, then slowed down.

"What else did the two of you talk about?"

"Juliet Fuller's murder," Clint said. "Some other things that weren't important—wait."

Clint stopped again, this time putting his hand on the sheriff's arm to stop him, as well.

"What?"

"She told me she exchanged slaps with Frank Cuddy yesterday, and he didn't like it."

"Slaps?" Sheriff Sheldon said. "You mean, to the face?" Clint nodded. "Yeah," said Sheldon. "I guess he wouldn't like that. You think he killed her because of it?"

"It's a hell of a reason to kill a woman," Clint said.

"That kid don't need much of a reason."

Once again they started to walk.

"Where is she?" Clint asked.

"One of the other girls found her behind the house," the sheriff said.

"How was she killed?"

"Strangled," the man replied, "like Miss Fuller."

"Damn," Clint muttered.

*　*　*

When they reached the back of the house, there were several women standing around, including Ginger. On the ground was a body covered by a blanket. When Ginger saw Clint, she ran to him and buried her face in his chest.

"He killed her," she sobbed. "That crazy kid killed her."

He held her tightly, then said softly, "I have to take a look, Ginger. Why don't you and the other ladies go into the house."

Ginger drew away from him and glared at the sheriff.

"You'd better arrest him, Sheriff," she said. "You better arrest him or I'll kill him myself."

She went and spoke to the other girls, and they all turned and went back into the house.

Clint walked over to the body and pulled the blanket back. Louisa was lying on her back, her face bloated, her head at an odd angle.

"Not only strangled," Clint said. "Her neck's been broken." He covered her up again, stood, and turned to face the sheriff. Beyond the lawman he could see several houses where the curtains were moving.

"They're watching us," Clint said. "You think they might have seen the murder?"

Sheldon turned and looked, and the curtains dropped.

"I guess I'll have to ask them," he said, looking back at Clint.

"You've got two murders on your hands, Sheriff," Clint said. "You can't ignore them."

"I don't intend to," Sheldon said, "but I told you I'm no detective, Adams. I could use your help."

"I'm not a detective, either."

"You told me you knew a detective," Sheldon said. "The best one in the business. You must've learned something from him. And you were gonna look into Miss Fuller's murder, anyway. Now you can look into two."

"We, Sheriff," Clint said. "We can look into two."

"That's what I meant."

TWENTY-FIVE

Clint remained with the body while the sheriff went to get some men to move it to the undertaker's office. When the lawman returned, he had the undertaker himself, Baron Giles, and two other men Clint had never seen before. One of them was wearing a deputy's badge.

"Clint, this is my new deputy, Hal Evans."

The deputy was a little older than Giles. He swallowed hard before nodding to Clint and saying, "Pleasure."

"These boys will all move her to Giles's office," Sheldon said to Clint.

"Good," Clint said, "I think we should talk to the people in those houses next."

"And then?" Sheldon asked.

"And then both Lincoln Town and his boy, Frank Cuddy," Clint said.

"I know Cuddy," Baron Giles said, anxiously. "I could help."

"How well do you know him?"

"We sorta grew up together," Giles said. "Or, at the same time, anyway."

Clint looked at Sheldon.

"Why not?" the sheriff said to Clint. He looked at Giles. "Get the body . . . get this lady over to your office, and we'll stop by and get you before we talk with Cuddy."

"Okay."

"You ready?" Sheldon asked. "Let's split up. We'll finish faster."

"I think we should go together," Clint said. "I've already talked to some of them about Juliet, and they weren't very helpful. Maybe if they see a badge, they'll be more inclined to talk."

"All right," Sheldon said.

As the three other men carried the body of Louisa away, Clint and the sheriff made their way over to the houses.

Despite the presence of Sheriff Sheldon's badge, the people in the houses didn't have any more to say than they had earlier when they spoke to Clint.

"The husbands are afraid to talk," Sheldon said as he and Clint left the last house. "They don't want their wives to know they might have been lookin' out the window at the back of the whorehouse."

Clint shook his head.

"I can't believe they could have watched while a woman was killed and not say anything."

"Maybe they'll come forward later, when their wives aren't standing there listenin'," the sheriff offered.

"I doubt it," Clint said. "You really want to take Giles with us to see Cuddy?"

"Like I said before, why not?" Sheldon said. "Let's see what he's made of when he faces somebody who's not afraid to use his gun on a man."

"You know, I never did ask," Clint said, "but you have seen Cuddy use his gun, haven't you?"

"Oh, yeah," Sheldon said. "I saw him gun down two men at once. He can use it, all right. Why, are you suddenly worried?"

"Just checking," Clint said.

They entered the undertaker's office and found Baron Giles waiting impatiently for them.

"We ready to go?" he asked.

"Did you take care of Louisa's body?"

"She's laid out in the back," he said. "I'll work on a marker later. You know when you want her buried?"

"She'd going to have a decent burial," Clint sad. "You've got a church here, right?"

"Yep," Sheldon said. "And a preacher."

"I'm sure Louisa's friends are all going to want to pay their respects."

"A funeral for a whore?" Giles asked. "I got to see that in this town."

"You're going to see it," Clint said. "Take off your gun belt."

"What?"

"Take off your gun belt," Clint said. "If you're coming with us, you're leaving your gun behind."

"But . . . why?"

"Because I don't know yet if you're a hothead or not," Clint said. "But I think you might be, and we're not ready for gunplay . . . not yet, anyway."

"I'll keep my gun in my holster," Giles promised.

"Well, we'll just make sure of that," Clint said. "Leave it, or you're not coming."

"What good will I be without my gun?" the younger man asked, removing the gun belt.

"I guess we'll find out, won't we?" Clint asked.

Giles walked over to his desk, opened a drawer, and put the gun belt inside. Clint liked that better than if Giles had simply tossed it aside. He was going to have to remind himself to examine the gun and see how well kept it was.

"Okay," Clint said, "let's go. Are we likely to find him at the Pat Hand?"

"That's as good a place as any," the sheriff said.

As they left the undertaker's office, Giles asked, "What are we gonna do, exactly?"

"Right now we're just going to ask some questions of both Lincoln Town and Cuddy," Sheldon said. "That is, Adams is gonna ask."

"Me? You're wearing the badge."

"You know what questions to ask," Sheldon said, "don't you?"

"We'll find out."

TWENTY-SIX

Clint entered the Pat Hand with Sheriff Sheldon and Baron Giles. The place was full, the music loud, and the liquor flowing. The girls barely had room to move between the patrons as they carried trays of drinks without spilling a drop. It seemed Lincoln Town only hired the best.

"The office," Sheldon said. "When it's this busy, he's usually in there."

"Lead the way," Clint said. "We'll need your badge to part the waters."

"What waters?" Giles asked.

Clint and the sheriff ignored him and the lawman led the way through the crowd until they reached the back door.

Sheldon knocked on the door and when Lincoln Town shouted something, he opened it. They all entered, single file, and Town looked up at them from his desk.

"Well, to what do I owe the pleasure of a visit from the Gunsmith, the sheriff and . . . is that the undertaker?"

"Baron Giles, sir," the young man replied.

Clint gave him a look and he shut up.

"Has someone died that I should know about?" Town asked.

"Yes, Town," Clint Adams said, "someone has died. One of the girls from the whorehouse was strangled to death today, just like Juliet Fuller."

The shocked look on Town's face was so convincing that Clint immediately believed it was sincere.

"Which one?"

"Louisa. She was the one—"

"Yes," Town said, holding up his hand. "I know which one she was." He looked at Sheldon. "What are you going to do about this, Sheriff?"

"I'm questioning likely suspects, Mr. Town."

"Then what are you doing here?"

"Like he said," Clint answered, "we're questioning likely suspects."

Town sat back in his chair.

"You suspect me of killing one of my own girls?"

"Why not?" Clint asked. "She made it very clear that she thought you killed Juliet, or had her killed."

"And I would kill her for that?" Town asked. "Who would take the word of a whore over mine?"

"That would be me," Clint said.

"Well," Town said, "let me just say for the record that I did not kill her, and since I'm not under arrest, you don't have evidence that I did."

"Where's your pet killer?" Clint asked.

"What? Who?"

"You know who," Clint said. "Cuddy."

"Frank Cuddy? I have no idea where he is." Town looked puzzled. "Why would I?"

"He works for you, doesn't he?"

"He has, from time to time," Town said. "At the moment I don't believe he's on my payroll."

Clint turned and looked at the sheriff, who shrugged.

"Where does he live?" Clint asked.

"And how would I know that?" Town asked. "All I know is that he sometimes mooches breakfast off my bartender in the morning."

"Do you know where he lives?" Clint asked the sheriff.

"No."

"I do."

Clint and Sheldon turned and looked at Baron Giles.

"He's in an old abandoned shack south of town," Giles said. "Been livin' there for years."

"You know where it is?" the lawman asked.

"Sure."

Clint turned and looked at Lincoln Town.

"We're not done," Clint said. "We're going to talk again."

"I look forward to it."

Clint turned and walked to the door. Sheldon followed, and Giles brought up the rear.

After they left, Lincoln Town sat back in his chair, steepled his fingers, and wondered if Frank Cuddy had finally snapped. If he had, and they found him at his shack, then he was sure to go out in a hail of bullets.

He wondered if Cuddy had secured that help yet.

Giles led Clint and the sheriff on foot south of town, to a clearing where a run-down shack stood—just barely.

"He lives there?" Clint asked.

Giles nodded and said, "At least, until it comes down around his head."

As the three of them started for the building, Giles suddenly stopped.

"What's wrong?" Clint asked.

"Let me go alone," the younger man said.

"Why?"

"Because I'm unarmed, and because he knows me," Giles said. "If he's there, he won't start shooting when he sees me."

"He's got a point," the sheriff said. "We only want to talk to him, but this could get ugly if he starts shooting."

"Okay," Clint said, figuring this was a good way for Baron Giles to prove himself.

Giles took a deep breath, then started walking toward Frank Cuddy's shack. As he got closer to it, he tensed, waiting for a bullet to rip through his body. When he reached the door without that happening, he breathed a sigh of relief and knocked.

"Frank," he called. "Frank Cuddy, it's Baron Giles."

No answer.

"Frank!"

He knocked again, being careful not to hit the door too hard for fear he'd knock it down.

He moved to one of the front windows and looked inside. There literally was no place for anyone to hide, so it was fairly obvious that it was empty.

He turned and waved at Clint and Sheldon to come ahead.

TWENTY-SEVEN

The front door was unlocked so there was no need to force it. The three men went inside. The shack was small, offering enough room for a bed, a table, a chair, and a potbelly stove that was probably used for heat as much as it was used for cooking.

"There's nothin' here," Sheldon said. "Maybe he's on the run."

"Or he's off doin' somethin' for Mr. Town," Giles offered.

"So he does work for Town on a regular basis?" the sheriff asked.

"Oh, yeah," Giles said. "He lied about that."

"The question is," Clint said, "did he go on an errand before or after killing Louisa?"

"Whichever it was, I guess we'll have to hope he comes back," the sheriff said.

"What if it's somebody else?" Giles asked.

Both Clint and the sheriff looked at him.

"I mean, what if there's some madman here in town killing whores?" he went on.

"Whoever it is," Clint said, "we're going to catch him."

They got out of there.

Walking back to town, Clint asked Sheriff Sheldon how many deputies he had.

"Just the one," the man said. "You met him earlier today. Hal Evans."

"I remember you telling me you didn't have any deputies."

"I just hired Hal yesterday."

"Does he have any experience?"

"No."

"Then why did you hire him?"

Sheldon made a face and said, "He's the son of the head of the town council."

"Why don't you give him a simple job, then?"

"Like what?"

"Like watching that shack and letting you know when Cuddy comes back."

"He'll get himself killed."

"He just has to stay out of sight and watch."

Sheldon thought about it, then said, "All right, that sounds simple enough."

"What's our next step?" Giles asked.

"Your next step is to go back to your place," Clint said. "You're done for the day."

"But—"

"You have to take care of Louisa," Clint said, cutting him off. "That's what you can do for me today."

Giles lowered his head, but said, "All right."

Clint looked at the sheriff.

"You want to get that deputy of yours situated?"

"Sure. What are you gonna do?"

"Talk to the girls," he said. "Maybe somebody saw something. Who found her?"

"I don't know," Sheldon said. "They sent somebody to fetch me, but I don't think she was the one who found her."

"Okay, I'll find out," Clint said. "I'll see you at your office a little later."

"Okay."

Clint turned and looked at Giles.

"I'm goin'," Giles said.

"So am I," Sheldon said. The sheriff and Giles walked back toward the center of town together, while Clint headed back to the house.

TWENTY-EIGHT

Clint found the front door unlocked when no one answered his knock. He walked in and found the entry hall empty. He wondered if all of the girls had gone upstairs, but he checked the drawing room first. He found three of them in there, including Ginger.

"Where are the rest of the girls?" he asked.

"They're in their rooms," Ginger told him.

"Keep that front door locked," Clint said. "You're inviting the killer to come inside."

"I think we'd all know Lincoln Town or Frank Cuddy if they came in."

"You may be convinced that they killed her," Clint said, "but we don't know that for a fact, yet."

"Do you know where that little killer is?" she demanded.

"No."

"See? He's on the run."

"Why would he run after killing Louisa when he didn't run after killing Juliet?"

"Because he knows you're after him this time."

"Ginger, I had coffee in town with Louisa before she was killed," he said. "Did she come back here at all?"

"No," Ginger said, "she never made it back. He must have caught her outside."

"I need to talk to the girls whose rooms overlook the back," he said. "Can you get them for me?"

"I'll go upstairs and get Holly and Bree, but you can talk to Linda while I'm doin' that. She's the girl over there on the divan."

"Okay, thanks."

As Ginger left the room, he walked over to the divan where a waiflike girl with pale skin and dark hair sat.

"Linda?"

She started and looked up at him. There was fear in her big, doe eyes.

"Relax," he said, "you're safe. My name is Clint Adams."

"Oh, yes, Ginger told me that you were Juliet's friend," she said.

"That's right. You have a room that overlooks the back of the house, don't you?"

"Yes, I do."

"You didn't happen to be looking out the window earlier today, did you?"

"N-no," she said. "I was asleep until I heard s-someone shouting."

"And who was that?" he asked. "Who found Louisa's body?"

"I think it was Holly."

"Okay, Linda, thank you."

As Clint turned, Ginger returned to the drawing room

with two other girls behind her. One had hair as blond as straw and barely concealed breasts. The other was a black girl who was holding her robe closed tightly.

"This is Holly," Ginger said, indicating the blonde, "and this is Bree."

"Holly," Clint said, "you found the body, right?"

"Yes, sir."

"Can we talk in the hall?" Clint asked. "Bree? Will you wait for me here?"

"Yes, sir."

He took Holly's arm and guided her out into the hall.

"I'm Clint."

"I know, Ginger told me."

"How did you come to find the body?"

"I just went out for a walk," she said. "I do that every day when I wake up."

"Did you happen to look out your window before you went?" he asked.

"Just to see what the weather was like."

"And you didn't see anyone?"

"No."

"Would you have been able to see the body from your window if it was there?"

"No," she said, "it was too close to the back of the house."

"So you what? Walked around the house and found it?"

"Yes," she said. "I don't like to go too far, so I just . . . walk around. When I got to the back and saw her, I started yelling."

"Did you know it was Louisa?"

"Yes," she said.

"You got close enough to see her face?"

"No," Holly said, "I just recognized her dress."

"And you didn't see anyone else around the house?" he asked. "In back, in the front?"

"No."

"Did you happen to look over at the other houses? Maybe see somebody at the window?"

"No, I didn't. I shouted and ran inside."

"Okay, Holly," he said. "Thanks. I wouldn't go for any morning walks for a while, though."

"Don't worry, I won't."

"You can go inside now."

"Can I just go back to my room?"

"Sure."

As she went back up the stairs, Clint returned to the drawing room, got the black girl, Bree, and also questioned her in the hall. She didn't know anything the other girls didn't, had not looked out her window at all that morning.

When Bree went back into the sitting room, Ginger came back out.

"Do you want to talk to anyone else?" she asked.

"No," he said, "nobody saw anything."

"So that means you can't do anything."

"I can keep asking questions.

"But . . . you're the Gunsmith," she said. "Can't you just . . . kill them? I could take up a collection so we can—"

"If you know anything about me from Juliet, you'd know I don't hire my gun out."

"I'm sorry," she said. "I'm just . . . upset. Juliet and Louisa were my best friends."

"I understand." He put his hand on her shoulder. "We're going to find out who killed them. Don't worry."

"I-I'll try.

He went to the door, opened it, and before going out said, "But keep this door locked."

TWENTY-NINE

When Clint got to the sheriff's office, he was happy to see a pot of coffee on top of the stove.

"You mind?"

"Be my guest," Sheldon said. He indicated that he already had a cup on his desk. "Any luck at the house? Anybody see anything?"

Clint sat across from the sheriff and sipped the coffee.

"This is a town of blind people," Clint said. "Nobody saw anything."

"What about the girl who found the body?"

"Went for a walk, recognized the woman's dress, started yelling," Clint said. "That was it."

"Nobody's got any ideas?"

"Oh, sure, they think it was Frank Cuddy, sent by Lincoln Town," Clint said. "They wanted to take up a collection to hire me to kill them."

"That'd be one way to solve it," Sheldon said.

"You saying you wish I'd taken that deal?" Clint asked.

"I'm the law, I can't say that," the lawman said. "I can think it, but I can't say it."

Sheldon took a whiskey bottle from his bottom drawer, held it up to Clint, who nodded and held out his coffee cup. The sheriff topped off Clint's coffee, then filled his own cup. Clint saw that there had been no coffee left in it.

"You got your deputy in place?" Clint asked.

"That kid," Sheldon said, shaking his head. "He ain't much of a deputy."

"Well, he can come and tell us when Cuddy gets back, right?" Clint asked. "There isn't much to that."

"I suppose he can do that." Sheldon's mood was close to morose. All it would take was a few more drinks.

"You aren't going to be much good the rest of the day if you keep drinking," Clint said.

Sheldon gave him a hard look, which quickly subsided. He stoppered the whiskey bottle, put it back in the desk, then pushed his coffee cup over to Clint's side of the desk.

"You're right," he said. "I'm lettin' this get to me."

"Why?" Clint asked. "Why this one and not the other?"

"No, I mean both of them," Sheldon said. "Maybe if I'd done something more after the first one, this one wouldn't have happened. You see what I mean?"

"I see," Clint said, and there was nothing he could say to make the man feel better. Not when he thought he was right.

Clint finished his coffee, then took both cups back over to the stove and set them aside. As an afterthought he took the sheriff's cup to the front door, opened it, and dumped the contents into the street, then came back in.

"Still got the bottle," Sheldon reminded him.

"I know," Clint said, replacing the cup, "but that'll be your responsibility." He turned and faced the sheriff. "What'd you think of the kid today?"

"Who? Giles?"

"Yeah, the undertaker."

"I thought he did okay," Sheldon said. "Showed some backbone walkin' up to that shack."

"Yeah," Clint said, "I thought so, too."

"Gonna use him?"

"Maybe," Clint said, "but I don't know what for."

"It's my guess that when Cuddy comes back, he'll come back with help," Sheldon said. "The kind of help that can use a gun. You're gonna need somebody to stand with you."

"What about you?"

"Me?" Sheldon shook his head. "I ain't no good. I been sheriff here for a long time, and ain't done much in all that time. Likely as not I'd get you killed. You need somebody who can use a gun."

"Guess I'll cross that bridge when I come to it, then."

"There is one thing I can do for you," the sheriff said.

"What's that?"

The man opened a drawer and for a moment Clint thought he was going to bring the bottle back out, but instead Sheldon tossed a tin star onto the desk.

"I can make you legal."

Clint waked to the desk, looked down at the star that read DEPUTY. Clint's first instinct was to say no, but then he thought better of it. He picked it up and put it in his shirt pocket.

"Not gonna pin it on?"

"That would make me an even bigger target than I am right now," Clint said. "I'll pull it out when I need it. I'm obliged."

"Might as well back you any way I can," Sheldon said. "I ain't gonna be much good for anything else."

"As long as you don't get in my way when I find the killer," Clint said, "we're going to be all square."

THIRTY

When Frank Cuddy rode back into town, he had four men with him. They were all of a kind—late twenties, early thirties, dirty trail clothes, worn holsters, cared-for guns.

Instead of heading for his shack, Cuddy took the four men right to the Pat Hand. They dismounted in front and entered the saloon. It was late afternoon and the place was just starting to fill up.

"Grab a table, boys," he told them. "I'll send some drinks over, on the house."

"This job is payin' off already," one of them said.

When Cuddy went to the bar, he told Artie, "Give 'em what they want, no charge."

"You got to clear that with the boss—"

"It's cleared," Cuddy said. "Just do it."

"Yeah, sure. Whiskey okay?"

"Yeah," Cuddy said, "a bottle."

"The boss wants to see you."

"Yeah? I wanna see him."

"Not as bad as he wants to see you."

"Why? What's goin' on?"

"Another one of them whores got herself killed."

"When?"

"This afternoon."

"How?"

"Way I hear it, same as the other one," Artie said. "Somebody choked her to death."

"And he thinks I did it?"

"Lots of people think you did it," Artie said, "includin' the law, and Clint Adams."

Artie came around from behind the bar and took the bottle over to the men Cuddy had brought in. Cuddy thought about getting himself a drink, then decided to go and talk to Town.

"Come!" Town yelled when Cuddy knocked.

As the gunman entered, Town demanded, "Where the hell have you been?"

"Doin' what you tol' me to do," Cuddy said. "I went and got us some help."

"Out of town?"

"That's right."

"When did you leave?"

"This afternoon."

"Before or after you killed that whore, Louisa?"

"Louisa? Which one's she?"

"You know which one she is," Town said. "She's the one who slapped the shit out of you."

"She's dead?" Cuddy asked. "Serves her right. Nothin' more of a waste than an old whore."

"Are you telling me you didn't kill her?" Town asked, leaning forward in his chair.

"Why would I kill 'er?" Cuddy asked. "You didn't tell me to. And if I was gonna kill 'er for slappin' me, I'da killed her on the spot."

Town sat back. It made sense to him.

"How many men did you bring back with you?"

"Four," Cuddy said. "They're all good boys."

"You tell them about Adams?"

"No," Cuddy said. "I didn't want anybody goin' off half-cocked. Adams is mine."

"You know the undertaker?"

"Baron? Yeah, I know him. Why?"

"He was with Adams and the sheriff when they came here and accused me of killing that whore."

"Was he wearin' his gun?" Cuddy asked.

"No, why? Is he good with it?"

"Outshoots me every year for a turkey," Cuddy said.

"He's better than you?"

"Hittin' a target," Cuddy said, "he's better than anyone I ever saw."

"And facing a man?"

"I don't know, and neither does he. He's never had to do it."

"Well, you may have to deal with him, too. Will that be a problem, you and him being friends?"

"I said I knew him," Cuddy said. "I didn't say nothin' about bein' friends."

"Where are your men?"

"Outside. I had Artie give 'em a bottle of whiskey on the house. He said I had to check with you."

"That's fine," Lincoln Town said, "but after that bottle— only beer. Got it?"

"I got it."

"Bring them in here one at a time so I can talk to them," Town said. "You tell them who would be paying them?"

"I did," Cuddy said. "I told them they were workin' for you."

"Good boy," Town said. "Bring them in, and stay out of sight for a while. The law's looking for you, and so is Clint Adams."

"Maybe I want him to find me."

"I'll tell you when you want him to find you," Town said. "Now bring them in.

THIRTY-ONE

Baron Giles happened to be looking out his front window when Frank Cuddy rode in with his new cohorts. He watched as they dismounted in front of the Pat Hand and went inside. Only then did he leave his office, lock it, and head for the sheriff's office.

Clint was about to leave the sheriff's office when the door opened and Baron Giles came rushing in.

"I saw him," he said breathlessly.

"Saw who?" Sheriff Sheldon asked.

"Frank Cuddy," Giles said. "He just come ridin' back to town."

"Where is he?" Clint asked.

"He went right to the saloon."

"Is he alone?" Sheldon asked.

"No," Giles said, "he's got four gunnies with him."

"Well," Clint said to the sheriff, "I guess you called that one right."

"I don't get any satisfaction out of it."

Clint headed for the door.

"Where are you going?" Sheldon asked.

"You might as well call your deputy off Cuddy's shack," Clint said. "I'm going to the saloon to talk to him."

"Alone?" the lawman asked.

Clint stopped, thought a moment, then said, "No, I'm taking the kid here with me."

"I'm wearin' my gun," Baron Giles said.

Clint looked at him, and said, "Kid, wouldn't have it any other way."

"Okay," Lincoln Town said to Frank Cuddy, "they'll do. Now you take them and get out of here."

"And go where?"

"To my other place."

Town had a small saloon in a less desirable part of town. It was called the No Name Saloon.

"The No Name? That place is a pit."

"Well, then, take them wherever you want, but get them out of here. I don't want them around until I need them."

"Fine," Cuddy said. "The No Name is as good a place as any. What about the free drinks?"

"No more free drinks," Town said. "There should be a bartender on duty named Willy. Tell him to charge you half price."

"How about food?"

"Get them fed in that part of town, put them up in that part of town," Town said. "What part of this don't you understand? I don't want them—or you—to be seen. I'll send for you when the time is right."

"Why do I have to hide out?"

"Because the sheriff may decide to arrest you for murder."

"Let him try."

"I don't want him to try," Town said. "Do you work for me?"

"Yes." *For now*, he added to himself.

"Then go and do what I told you to do—and take them out the back."

"Okay," Cuddy said, "but I hope this won't go on for too long. I promised these guys some action."

"Believe me," Town said, "I think the Gunsmith will be only too happy to give you all the action you want."

"Any action comin' from the Gunsmith is gonna be mine," Cuddy said, leaving the office.

Rex Stokes saw Frank Cuddy come out of his boss's office looking none too happy.

"Looks like we're gettin' kicked out," he said to the other men at the table.

"Aw, I knew it was too good to be true," Scott Parker said. "Think we got time for one more free drink?"

John Witt turned in his chair and looked at Cuddy.

"I doubt it," he said, shaking his head. "Not judging from the look on his face."

Cuddy reached the table and said to them, "Come on, we're out of here."

"Where are we goin'?" Stokes asked.

"Another saloon."

"Why?"

"The boss don't want us seen around here."

Chairs scraped the floor as the four men stood up.

"We still gonna get free drinks?" Scott Parker asked.

"Half-price drinks," Cuddy said.

Stokes slapped Parker on the back and said, "Almost as good, Scott, almost as good."

THIRTY-TWO

No one was more disappointed than Baron Giles to find that Frank Cuddy was not in the Pat Hand.

"Come on," Clint said to the kid and led him over to the bar.

"Help ya?" Artie asked.

"Where's Cuddy?" Clint asked.

"Whataya mean?"

"I mean I'm going to be very displeased with you if you don't give me an answer the second time I ask the question," Clint said, giving the man a hard stare.

"Artie," Giles said, "I'd answer him if I was you. This here's the Gunsmith."

"Frank Cuddy was in here," Clint said.

"I saw him," Giles offered.

"He's not in here now," Clint added. "What I want to know is, where did he go?"

Artie swallowed hard, looked at Giles imploringly.

"Baron, I could get in a lotta trouble."

"Artie," Giles said, "you could get dead."

Artie looked at Clint with fear in his eyes.

"Mister, honest, all I know is he was here and then he left by the back door. I don't know where he went."

"Who was with him?"

"Four men."

"You know them?"

"Never saw 'em before."

"What were they doing in here?"

"They was drinkin' for free."

"And?"

Artie swallowed again, then wet his lips.

"They each went in and talked to the boss."

"What was he doing?" Clint asked. "Interviewing them for jobs?"

"Honest, I dunno."

Clint believed him.

"Two beers, Artie," he said.

"Yes, sir."

"Why are we drinkin' here?" Giles asked.

"Two reasons," Clint said. "I want Lincoln Town to see us in here."

"And the second reason?"

"I'm thirsty."

Lincoln Town came out of his office and saw Clint and Giles drinking at the bar. He was tempted to go back in, but decided to brazen it out. Besides, this was his place.

He walked up to the bar and knew by the way the bartender was avoiding his gaze that Artie had told Clint Adams something.

"Adams," he said. "Back again?"

"I got thirsty," Clint said. "I was told you serve the best beer in town."

"You were told right," Town said. "Artie?"

"Yes, sir?" Artie looked at his boss guiltily.

"Mr. Adams and Mr. Giles's beers are on the house."

"Yes, sir."

"What's wrong, Artie?"

"Uh, nothin's wrong, boss," Artie said. "Nothin' at all."

"You look like you've got a guilty conscience."

"Me? Whatta I got to feel guilty about?"

"I don't know."

"Maybe he feels guilty about telling us were we can find Frank Cuddy," Clint offered.

"I didn't—" Artie sputtered. "I never—"

"Relax, Artie, relax," Town told him. "I know you didn't." He looked at Clint and smiled. "Nice try, Adams, but Artie doesn't know where Frank is."

"Well, maybe you do."

"Sorry," Town said. "Like I told you before, I have no idea."

"Well, he was in here a few minutes ago," Baron Giles said.

"Was he?"

"I saw him come in."

"Artie, was Frank Cuddy in here?"

"Uh, yeah, boss. He was . . . for a while, but then he left."

"Well, there you go," Town said to Clint. "He was here but now he's not. What else do you need to know?"

"Well," Clint said, "for one thing I'd like to know how you had the gall to step in and take over Juliet Fuller's business after her death?"

"Gall?" Town asked. "I did that out of the goodness of my heart, Adams. Those women would be out on the street if I hadn't."

"They don't seem so grateful to you, Town," Clint said. "In fact, most of them don't seem to like you."

"How do you figure that?" Town asked. "I did them a favor and they don't like me. Maybe I should just let the business go to hell and allow them to end up on the street."

"I'm sure that business can survive without you."

Town smiled.

"No, I think I'll hold on to it for a while," he said. "It's really doing quite well."

"You have no legal right to it."

"I'll just wait for someone with some official standing to tell me that, if you don't mind."

Clint took the deputy's badge from his pocket and asked, "Is this official enough for you?"

Town looked surprised, but recovered.

"I'm afraid a deputy just doesn't do it for me, Mr. Adams," he said. "I was thinking more along the lines of a judge."

"Well," Clint said, "I guess I'll go and have a conversation with the local judge."

"Do that," Lincoln Town said, "and give Judge King my best. We're very good friends." He looked at Artie. "Let them have all the beer they want, Artie."

"No, thanks," Clint said, setting his unfinished mug down, "all of a sudden it tastes very flat."

THIRTY-THREE

"Where would I find this Judge King?" Clint asked Giles when they were outside.

"His office or his home."

"You know where both are?"

"Yep."

"Let's start with his office. Lead the way."

"You're not gonna have much luck with Judge King," Giles said as they were walking.

"Why not?"

"Lincoln Town owns him."

"I figured as much, but I'd like to talk to him, anyway."

"Suit yourself."

"What'd you tell them, Artie?" Town asked his bartender.

"He was gonna kill me, Mr. Town."

"He wouldn't have shot you in cold blood."

"How do you know? He's a killer, ain't he?"

"Just tell me what you told him, word for word."

Artie repeated the conversation as he remembered it. Town listened without comment until the end.

"Okay," he said, "no harm done. But Artie?"

"Yeah?"

"I have the feeling if you had known where Cuddy was you would have told Adams."

"Aw, Mr. Town—"

"Just remember who pays you," Town said. "And don't make me have to tell Frank that you were ready to give him up."

Artie's eyes went wide. "Boss, he's crazy. He'd kill me."

"Yes," Town said, "he would."

Clint and Giles reached a brick building in the center of town. Above the doorway it read CITY HALL.

"The judge has an office here?"

Giles nodded, said, "And it's bigger than the mayor's."

"How does the mayor feel about that?"

"He feels however the judge tells him to feel."

"So Town owns the judge and the judge owns the mayor?" Clint asked.

"That's the way it seems to me."

"Who owns the town council?"

"I don't think I've ever been to a meeting," Giles said. "I'm not even sure who's on it."

They tried the judge's office and found it locked.

"Okay," Clint said. "His home next."

"He won't like bein' bothered at home," Giles said as they left City Hall. "And neither will his wife."

"Too bad."

The judge's house stood alone just outside of town and looked like it belonged in the South. It had four white columns in front, was two stories high, and was probably worth more than the entire town.

"If a black man wearing white gloves answers the door . . ." Clint said.

"What?"

"Forget it."

The door was answered by a stern-looking, white-haired woman in her early sixties.

"My husband is not home," she said. "Check his office."

"We did that, ma'am," Clint said. "It's very important that I speak to him. Do you have any idea where else he might be?"

"Well," she said, with a sigh, "check the whorehouse, then. The randy old son of a bitch is probably there."

She slammed the door in their faces.

"That's quite a woman," Clint said.

"Scares everybody in town," Giles said.

Clint smiled at Giles and said, "I like her."

THIRTY-FOUR

Regina opened the door to Clint and Giles.

"Where were you this afternoon?" Clint said, pushing his way in.

"What do you mean?"

"I mean when Louisa was getting killed," Clint said. "When her body was being found."

"I went out early to do some shopping," she said. "Why do I have to account for myself to you?"

He took out the deputy's badge for the second time that day and hoped he wouldn't end up feeling silly again.

"This is why."

"You're the law now?" she asked, surprised.

"That's right."

"Well . . . what do you want now?"

"Judge King."

"What about him?"

"Is he here?"

"Uh, yes," she said. "He's upstairs with Bree."

"The black girl?"

"That's right," Regina said. "The judge always asks for her."

"Which room is Bree's?" Clint asked.

"Nine."

Clint started up the stairs.

"We're not even open yet," she called up. "The other girls are all gettin' ready."

"We'll try not to disturb them."

They got to the second floor and Clint led the way to room nine, then turned to Giles.

"You want to wait out here?"

"Why?"

"Because when I leave here, you still have to live in this town," Clint said. "Maybe you don't want to get on the wrong side of Judge King."

"I've spent too many years tryin' not to get on the wrong side of people," Giles said. "Maybe it's time I spent some time on that side."

"Okay," Clint said, and opened the door.

Judge King looked down at the young black girl between his legs, working away at his cock with her mouth, trying in vain to get it hard. His wife knew he came here and didn't care because she hated sex. He liked it, but what she didn't know was that it had been a long time since one of these whores had been able to get him hard. But this sweet young negro girl had come closest the last two times, and he thought if he kept coming to her, eventually she'd do the trick. He just wanted to feel his hard dick inside a woman once more before he died—or, at least, before he turned seventy, which was in two more years.

And then, suddenly, it was happening.

"Oh, yeah, you sweet young thing," he said, "it's workin', I can feel it—"

"Mmm-hmmm," she said, with her mouth full.

He was getting hard, he was! She was sucking on him now, like he was a whole man again.

"Get on up here, girl, and climb aboard," he said, reaching for her . . . and then the door opened and two men came barging in.

"What in the Sam Hill—" he shouted, his erection going down fast as the girl released him and sat back on the bed.

"Oh, judge," Clint said, "that's just pitiful."

THIRTY-FIVE

"You can go, Bree," Clint said to the girl. "The judge is finished with you now."

She got off the bed and reached for her dress. He saw that she had flawless skin and small breasts with dark chocolate-colored nipples.

"He ain't paid yet."

"Where are his pants?"

She pointed to a chair. Clint walked over, got the judge's wallet out, and tossed a few bills to Bree.

"Hey," the judge shouted, as she went out the door, "that's too much—"

Clint tossed the judge his pants and said, "Get dressed, Your Honor. We got some talking to do."

"Who the hell are you?" Judge Hiram King demanded.

"My name's Clint Adams, Judge."

"Adams," the older man pulled on his pants, then grabbed his shirt and covered his sagging flesh with it. "I heard you were in town." He looked at Giles. "I know you?"

"This is your local undertaker."

"I knew I knew you," King said, pulling on his boots. "Henry Giles's boy."

"You about done?"

The judge stood up, and Clint was surprised to see that the old man stood straight and tall, a good six-four. There was no stoop to him yet.

"Who the hell are you and what do you want?" the judge asked. Now that he was dressed he didn't look—or feel—quite as silly.

"My name is Clint Adams, Judge," Clint said. "I'm here in town trying to find out who killed Juliet Fuller and a woman named Louisa." Clint felt bad, but at that moment he didn't remember Louisa's last name, or if he even ever knew it.

"The two whores who were killed?" the judge asked.

"That's right."

"What's your interest?"

"Well, Juliet was a friend of mine," Clint said, "and my interest in Louisa's murder is to make sure it doesn't happen to anybody else."

"Why does that mean that you can barge in on me while I'm, uh, consulting?"

"Judge," Clint said, "somebody in this town has to care about what happened to these women."

"Why?" King asked. "They're whores."

"You're in a whorehouse," Clint said, "and you were just with a whore."

"One has nothing whatsoever to do with the other," the judge announced. "Excuse me."

He pushed past Clint out into the hall and started down the stairs. Giles looked at Clint helplessly, and then both men followed the judge down and out onto the street.

"How did you know I was here?" the judge demanded.

"Your wife told me," Clint said.

The judge stopped short and asked, "What?"

"She told me you were a randy old bastard and were probably here."

Clint expected the judge to get angry but the man actually seemed to like being called either "randy" or an "old bastard."

He started walking again, heading back to the center of town and the city hall building. Clint and Giles flanked him.

"Why are you bothering me with this?" the judge asked. "Take it to the sheriff."

"I have," Clint said.

"And?"

"We've narrowed the suspects down to two."

"Who are they?"

"Frank Cuddy and the man he works for, Lincoln Town."

The judge frowned and increased his pace.

"That's preposterous," he said. "Lincoln Town is a respected businessman and member of the community."

"He had Juliet Fuller killed so he could take over her business, which he did."

"He rescued a business that was going under, and he kept those poor girls from having to work on the streets."

"I want you to make a ruling and force him to give the business up," Clint said.

"Why would I do that?"

"Because he has no legal right to it."

"Can you prove that?"

"Yes."

"Good," the judge said, "write up a brief and have it on my desk and I'll rule on it."

"I can't write a brief."

"Then you better get yourself a lawyer. I will only rule on a legally drawn up brief."

They reached city hall and the judge finally stopped. Clint realized he was breathing hard from trying to keep up with the older man.

"Anything else?"

Clint hesitated, then said, "No, nothing else."

"Then good day."

The judge went into the building.

"Why didn't you show him your badge?" Giles asked.

"Because I haven't been duly sworn in," Clint said. "The sheriff just gave me the badge to help me out."

"Then why not get sworn in?" Giles asked.

"You know," Clint said, "that's not such a bad idea, Baron. For both of us."

"What? Me a deputy?"

"Maybe," Clint said. "I'll talk to the sheriff about it. Meanwhile, I need a lawyer. Are there any in town?"

"One that I know of," Giles said.

"Where's his office?"

"I'll take you there," Giles said, "but I don't know how happy you'll be with him."

"Why?"

"You'll see."

THIRTY-SIX

"That's him?" Clint asked.

"That's him," Giles said.

They were in a small saloon that, as far as Clint could tell, had no name. It was on a side street, small and dingy, with puddles on the floor that he hoped were from whiskey or beer. They were looking at a man who was sitting at a table with his head down on it—in a puddle of what Clint hoped was beer or whiskey.

"What's his name?" Clint asked.

"Well, his name is Raymond Olson, but everybody calls him Sudsy. At least, they have been for the past few years."

"Because his drink of choice is beer?" Clint asked.

Giles nodded.

"That's not very original. What happened?"

"His wife died," Giles said. "Some kind of fever took her. Up until that point he was a respected lawyer in town."

"Jesus," Clint said. "A drunk who actually has a good reason. Does he know you?"

"Oh, yeah. I took care of his wife, uh, after . . . well, after."

"Of course you did," Clint said. "Well, can we sober him up long enough to write a brief?"

"Honestly," Giles said, "I ain't sure."

"I guess we'll have to try."

They approached the table and the smell of beer convinced Clint that at least the puddle the man was face-down in was beer.

"How does he not drown in that?" he asked.

"I think his skin just absorbs it," Giles said.

"Let's sit him up."

They each grabbed an arm and straightened the man up. As he hit the back of the chair, his head lolled over to one side and a string of drool dripped out.

"Find out from the bartender how long he's been here and how much he's had to drink."

"Right."

As Giles walked away, Clint slapped the man's cheeks lightly, then harder. He was about to hit him again, when he saw the drunk's eyes flutter.

"Hey, Raymond? Can you hear me?"

"Of course I can hear you," Raymond Olson said belligerently, "I'm not deaf."

Clint guessed Olson was about fifty, and from the way his clothes hung on him Clint also guessed that the man had lost a lot of weight since the death of his wife.

Giles came back from the bar and said, "The bartender says the beer he's lyin' in was his first."

"So he's not drunk?"

"Bartender says he came in and ordered a beer, then went to sleep with his head on the table. I guess he hasn't been sleepin' much."

"Baron, is that you?" Raymond Olson asked, squinting up at the undertaker.

"It's me, Uncle Ray."

"How are you, boy?" Olson said. "I don't see much of you these days."

"You don't see much of anything these days, Uncle Ray."

"Uncle?" Clint asked.

Giles nodded.

"My mother was an Olson."

Olson rubbed his face and looked around him.

"Must've fallen asleep."

"Facedown in your first beer of the day, apparently," Clint said.

"Well," Olson said, "we can remedy that. Bartender!"

"No, no," Clint said, "no beer yet. Bartender, you got any coffee?"

"Comin' up."

"Make it three. Come on, let's move to another table."

He grabbed Olson's arm but the lawyer pulled away.

"Who's your pushy friend, Baron?"

"This is Clint Adams," Giles said. "The Gunsmith, Uncle Ray. You've heard of him."

"Of course I've heard of him. What's he doin' with you?"

"He's my friend," Giles said, "and he needs a lawyer."

"A lawyer?" Olson asked. "I haven't practiced law for years."

"But you haven't forgotten it, right?" Clint asked.

The man looked up at Clint.

"I suppose that depends on what kind of law we're talkin' about," Olson said.

"Can we move to another table and discuss it?" Clint asked.

Raymond Olson looked down at the puddle of beer on the table and then made a face.

"Disgusting," he said. "By all means let us repair to another table. One without disgusting liquids on it."

Including, Clint added to himself, *lawyer Raymond Olson's own drool.*

THIRTY-SEVEN

They took the coffee over to a clean table and the three of them sat down.

"Sir," Raymond Olson said, "if you're lookin' for a lawyer, you are lookin' in the wrong place. My nephew can even tell you—"

"You're nephew is the one who brought me to you, Mr. Olson," Clint said. "What I need is fairly simple for a lawyer."

"And what would that be?"

Clint explained what he needed and why.

"Judge King said that?"

"Yes," Clint said, "why? Is that odd?"

"Well, yes, for two reasons. The first is that Lincoln Town is clearly not entitled to take over that business."

"And the second?"

"He knows that I'm the only lawyer in town," Olson said. "Clearly he has no intention of making the ruling you want."

"Can you write this brief?" Clint asked.

"When I am sober, yes," Olson said, "but I don't intend to be sober for very long."

"Longer than you think," Clint said. He looked at Giles. "You've been wanting to help, now's your chance. Sit on him and keep him sober until he has that brief written."

"B-but I don't want to write the brief," Olson complained. "I want a drink."

"No more drinks until that brief is written," Clint told the man.

"You can't do that!"

"And I'll pay you."

Now a crafty look came into the man's eyes and for the first time he looked like a lawyer.

"How much?"

"We'll discuss it when you're done," Clint said. "That's the deal. Money, and a drink, after you've written the brief."

"Judge King will ignore it."

"That's okay," Clint said. "You just write the damn thing and I'll handle the judge."

"You can do it, Uncle Ray," Giles said.

"Can you do it?" Clint asked Giles. "Keep him sober 'til he's done?"

"Don't worry, Clint," Giles said. "You can depend on me and my uncle."

Clint got directions to the man's law office and told them he'd meet them later that evening.

In the back of the No Name Saloon a poker game was going on. The participants were Frank Cuddy and his new friends. Cuddy was the youngest, but he was clearly the leader, just as he was clearly the better poker player.

After he'd taken yet another hand, Rex Stokes asked, "So when are we gonna find out what's goin' on, Frank?"

"Hey," Scott Parker asked, "what's your hurry, Rex? Right now we're gettin' paid to play poker."

"Yeah," John Witt asked, "what's wrong with that?"

The fourth man looked around the table and said, "I wouldn't mind some action."

They all looked at him. He was the one they knew the least. In fact, the others didn't know him at all. Only Frank Cuddy did. The man's name was Theo Feathers.

"And don't make fun of his last name," Cuddy had warned the others. "He don't like it. And he's better with a gun than any of you."

"Better than you?" Stokes had asked.

"Nobody is better than me," Cuddy had replied.

Now they all looked at Feathers.

"I'm getting tired of sitting around and doing nothing," he said. "I need some action. I need to earn my money."

"The kid is right," Stokes said, because Feathers was the same age as Cuddy. "Whataya say, Frank?"

"What can I tell you, Rex?" Cuddy asked. "I got a boss and he calls the shots, understand? And right now he wants us to sit here and wait."

"And drink at half price," Witt said. "Don't forget that."

"This swill?" Feathers asked. "I'm done drinking this."

"Yeah," Stokes said, again siding with Feathers. "This'll kill us before we get to do our job."

"Well," Parker said, "beer's beer to me and I'm gettin' another one. Anybody else want one?"

"Bring me one," John Witt said.

"Comin' up," Scott Parker said. He left the back room and entered the saloon.

When they had all entered, they'd seen the man with his head down on the table and assumed, like everyone else did, that he was drunk. Now there was a young guy helping him up.

"Good idea, kid," Parker shouted. "Get him out of here before he drowns."

Parker had left the door to the back room open when he came out. When Giles turned to see who was talking, he saw past the man into the room, where Frank Cuddy was playing poker with a bunch of men.

THIRTY-EIGHT

Clint decided to go back to the house and check on the women. When he knocked, the door was opened by the black girl, Bree.

"Hello, Bree."

"Hello, mister."

"My name is Clint."

"Hello, Clint."

"Where is Regina?"

Bree shrugged.

"How about Ginger? Do you know where she is?"

"She's inside."

"Can I come in?"

"You wanna go upstairs with me?"

"No, Bree, thanks," Clint said. "I just want to talk to Ginger."

Without a word Bree turned and walked away, leaving the door open. Clint entered, closing the door behind him. He checked the drawing room and didn't see Ginger, so he decided to try the little office off the entryway. He found her there, going through the drawers of a desk. He didn't say anything, but she jumped as if he'd startled

her. She was not dressed to greet gentleman callers, but
was wearing a shirt and trousers.

"Oh, God," she said, putting her hand to her chest, "I
thought you were Lincoln."

"Do all the girls call him by his first name?" Clint
asked.

"He told us to, but some do, some don't," she said, going back to the desk.

"What are you looking for?"

She straightened up and looked at him helplessly.

"I thought I might find . . . something from Juliet."

"Like a will?"

"I don't think she would have made a will," Ginger
said. "Why would she? She didn't expect to get killed. But
yeah, something like that, I guess . . . just something that
would help us get this place away from Lincoln Town."

"I'm working on that right now," he said, and told her
about his conversations with Judge King and the lawyer,
Raymond Olson.

"You really think you're gonna be able to get it away
from him legally?" she asked.

"I'm going to try everything, Ginger," he said. "How
are the girls doing?"

"I think they're in shock," she said. "First Juliet and
now Louisa. I think they're wonderin' who's gonna be
next? None of them want to go outside."

"That doesn't seem to bother Regina. Where is she?"

"I don't know," Ginger said, frowning. "She does sort
of go in and out a lot."

"Do you think she goes and reports to Lincoln Town
on what goes on here?"

"It wouldn't surprise me," Ginger said. "He had to put
her in charge for a reason, didn't he?"

"I'm sure he did," Clint said. "Well, I'll leave you to your search." He started to leave, then stopped. "Does Lincoln Town ever use this desk?"

She straightened from her work again.

"I've never seen him even sit at it," she said. "He doesn't actually come here that often."

"Why would he?" Clint asked. "He's got Regina watching the place for him. I'll see you later."

"Clint?"

"Yes?"

"Do you think we could have someone watch the house?" she asked. "It might make some of the girls feel better."

From the look on her face it would make her feel better, as well. Clint thought briefly about Sheriff Sheldon's young deputy.

"I'll talk to the sheriff about it," he said, "but maybe I'll move my things over here from the hotel so I can spend the nights here."

"That would be great," she said. "You could use . . . Louisa's room."

"I'll be back later, then."

He turned to leave and she went back to searching the desk.

After Clint left the house, he walked to the sheriff's office. He was surprised to not find the sheriff there, since he'd been there every other time. He did, however, find the deputy, Hal Evans, sitting behind the sheriff's desk. The young man jumped up as if he'd been caught at something.

"Trying it out for size?" Clint asked.

"I was just—"

"Don't get up on my account."

"I, uh—the sheriff's not here."

Clint wondered if the young man had his eye on getting the top job through his father's influence.

"When will he be back?"

"I, uh, ain't sure."

"Well, I'll tell you what I want," Clint said, "and you can pass it on to him."

"Oh, okay."

"I'm going to move my gear out of the hotel and into the whorehouse, so the girls will have somebody there at night."

"Okay."

"But I'd like to have somebody outside the house during the day," Clint said.

"I could do that," the young man said anxiously.

"Well, that's what I was thinking, but I wanted to check with the sheriff first."

"I'll do it," Evans said. "But I'll, uh, check it with him first."

"Okay," Clint said, "but if he says no, let me know. I'll find somebody else."

Clint turned and walked to the door.

"Mister Adams . . ."

He turned with his hand on the knob.

"Yeah?"

"If he says no, I'll do it anyway."

Clint smiled and said, "You're a good man."

THIRTY-NINE

Clint left the sheriff's office and walked to the law office of Raymond Olson. The door was open so he entered, found Baron Giles standing over his uncle, who was sitting with his head in his hands.

"I need a drink," he said, as Clint closed the door.

"Sorry, Uncle Ray," Giles said. "Clint said no drink until you're finished."

Clint was kind of surprised that the kid was sticking to his guns.

"Look at my hands," Ray Olson said, holding them out. Clint saw them shaking uncontrollably. "I can't write—" He stopped short when he saw Clint. He held his hands out even further. "Look!"

"I see," Clint said. He looked at Giles. "Does he have a bottle in here?"

"I'm sure he does."

"Where is it, Ray?" Clint asked.

"In the filing cabinet."

Giles went over and got out a bottle of rotgut whiskey that was about a quarter full.

"Just two fingers," Olson said, "that's all I need."

"Give him one," Clint said.

Giles found a dirty glass on top of the cabinet, measured out one finger of whiskey, and handed the glass to Clint.

"This should stop your hands from shaking," Clint said, holding the glass out to Olson. "Once you finish the brief, you can have as much as you want."

Olson grabbed the glass like a drowning man and downed it quickly.

"One more," he said to Clint, handing him the empty glass.

"No."

"Son of a bitch," Olson said. "You got no right."

"You're right," Clint said, "I don't, and I'm sorry, but I need you to do this for me."

Olson wiped his sweaty brow on his jacket sleeve, then stood up and took the jacket off. He tossed it aside, rolled up his shirtsleeves, sat back down, and started to write. Clint called Giles aside.

"Is he going to make it?" he asked.

"He'll do it," Giles said. "I'm sure of it."

"Okay," Clint said. "I've made arrangements for the deputy to watch the whorehouse until tonight, when I'm going to move there from the hotel."

"Stayin' in the whorehouse overnight?" Giles asked. "Can't beat that. They got a room for me?"

"They've got a lot of rooms for you," Clint said, "all you have to do is pay for one."

"Great," Giles said, "you mean just like always."

"You've been to the whorehouse?" Clint asked.

"Ain't many men in town who haven't been there."

"You're probably right," Clint said. "All right, when he's done, come and find me."

"Where will you be?"

"Moving my gear out of the hotel, making sure somebody's watching the house."

"Oh, before you go," Giles said as Clint headed for the door, "there's somethin' I think you should know."

"What's that?"

"Frank Cuddy is over at the saloon where we found Uncle Ray," he said.

"What?"

"There's a back room where they play poker," Giles explained. "As I was leavin' with Uncle Ray, the door opened and a man came out. I saw Cuddy sitting at the poker table with three others."

"Five altogether?"

"That's right."

"When were you going to tell me this?"

"I just did."

Clint thought a moment.

"There's no telling if they'll still be there."

"It was my impression," Giles said, "they were killin' time. You know, waitin'."

"Waiting for word from Lincoln Town, no doubt," Clint said. "Well, I want to talk to Cuddy."

"So you're goin' over there?"

"Right from here."

"You shouldn't go alone," Giles said. "Not with five of them. Anythin' could happen."

The kid had a point.

"You want to go with me?"

"Oh, yeah."

"Okay," Clint said, "finish up here with your uncle. I'll come back and get you. If you're right and they are waiting, they'll probably still be there."

"They were drinkin'," Giles said, "so if they're still there, they'll be liquored up."

Clint poked Giles in the chest and said, "That's a good observation, kid. I'll see you in a little while."

FORTY

Clint went back to the jailhouse to see if the sheriff had returned, and he was there.

"Your deputy talk to you?" Clint asked.

"Yeah, he did," Sheldon said. "He's over at the house now. I hope they don't corrupt him. I'd have a lot to explain to his father if that happens."

"I'll be over there soon enough and I'll let him go with his virtue intact," Clint promised.

"Did you find Cuddy?"

"Found him, but haven't talked to him yet."

"Where is he?"

"Some little saloon with no name," Clint said, "playing poker in the back room."

"I know the place," the sheriff said. "In fact, it's owned by Lincoln Town."

"Really? I wonder how he got his hands on that one?" Clint asked. "For that matter, how did he get the Pat Hand?"

"I don't know," Sheldon said. "He just showed up one day as the owner."

"What about the previous owner?"

"Just . . . gone."

"Okay, well, I'm going over to the saloon after I run some errands, and the kid is coming with me."

"Giles? The undertaker?"

"That's right. Cuddy's got four men with him."

"If they been sittin' in a saloon all day, they're gonna be drunk," Sheldon said.

"I know," Clint said. "Giles already pointed that out."

"Could end up in gunplay."

"If it does, it'll accomplish half my goal."

"Lincoln Town bein' the other half?"

"That's right."

"If you kill them—"

"Don't worry," Clint said. "It won't come back on you."

"I might have to arrest you."

Clint gave the man a level stare and said, "You might have to try."

The sheriff tried to hold Clint's stare, but in the end he had to look away.

Clint went to the hotel, collected his gear, checked out, and walked over to the whorehouse. Ginger let him in and took him up to Louisa's room. He looked around for Deputy Evans, but didn't see him. He hoped the young man was hiding somewhere, watching the house and waiting for the killer to show.

As he followed Ginger upstairs, he asked, "Have you seen the deputy I sent over to watch the house?"

"No," she said, "not a sign. Where is he supposed to be?"

"He probably found a good spot to keep himself out of sight," Clint said.

When they got to Louisa's room, he put his saddlebags over a chair and set his rifle down in a corner.

"Has Regina come back yet?" he asked.

"No."

"I didn't see her in town."

"Do you think something happened to her?"

"Probably not," he said. "She's probably with Lincoln Town, making some kind of report to him."

"I don't like Regina," Ginger said, "but I don't want any more girls ending up dead."

"I'm sure she's okay," Clint said. "I'll see if I can find her."

She walked him downstairs and he made sure she locked the door before he left.

FORTY-ONE

Clint didn't want to worry Ginger, but he was also wondering if something had happened to Regina. He kept his eyes peeled for her as he walked back to Ray Olson's law office.

When he entered, he saw Baron Giles sitting at his uncle's desk.

"What happened? Where is he?"

"He's in the back room with his bottle."

"Did he get it—" Clint started to ask, but then Giles held up a sheaf of papers.

"He did it," Clint said, taking the papers.

"He did something," Giles said. "I don't know if it's any good."

"I guess we'll find out tomorrow, when we take it to the judge," Clint said. "Right now we're going back to that No Name Saloon."

"I'm ready." Giles stood up.

"Hold on a minute, Baron," Clint said. "Sit back down."

"This ain't where you tell me I got to take off my gun again, is it?" the younger man asked.

"No, no," Clint said, "you can keep your gun on."

Giles sat back down.

"You've never fired your gun at a man, have you?"

Giles hesitated, then said, "No, I haven't."

"Do you think you can?"

"Yes," he said, without hesitation.

"You don't want to think about that before you answer?" Clint asked.

"No."

"Just like that?"

"If somebody is shootin' at me," Giles said, "I can shoot at them. It's that easy."

Clint didn't think it was that easy, but he didn't say anything about it.

"Okay, then," he said. "Let's go."

Giles stood up and said to Clint, "There's one more thing I should tell you."

"What's that?"

"I've been thinkin' about what I saw in that back room," Baron Giles said, "and I'm pretty sure I saw Feathers back there."

"Feathers?" Clint asked. "Bird feathers?"

"Theo Feathers," Giles said. "He's about the same age as Cuddy and me, and he's better with a gun. Well, faster."

"Faster than Cuddy?"

Giles nodded and said, "Frank would tell you no, but I've seen both their moves. He is."

"What about you?" Clint asked. "Is he faster than you?"

"No," Giles said, then, "well, yes, he's faster, but my first shot always counts."

"And his doesn't?"

Giles shook his head. "He rushes too much, sometimes."

"You know this for a fact?"

"Yes."

Clint was impressed with Baron Giles for the first time since meeting him. If he was correct, this was valuable information.

"You didn't recognize anyone else?

"No."

"Not even the man who came out for drinks?"

"No."

"Did he speak?"

"Yes," Giles said, and told Clint what the man had said about Uncle Ray.

"Okay," Clint said, "now the big question. If somebody goes for their gun, can you handle Cuddy while I handle Feathers?"

"Yes."

"And what about the others?"

"What about them?"

"There will be three more," Clint said. "Can you stay calm under fire?"

He was glad to see the young man hesitate before answering.

"I don't know," Giles said, "but I've always wanted to find out."

"Well, you might get your chance," Clint said. "When we walk in there, if they're drunk enough, somebody's going to panic and go for their gun. We want to try to avoid that."

"How do we do that?"

"Listen up . . ."

Of the five men playing poker in the back room of the No Name Saloon, only Cuddy and Feathers were not drunk.

"Boys," Cuddy said, "I think it might be time for you to stop drinkin' and sleep it off."

"Anybody know what time it is?" Stokes asked. "Must be dark out by now."

"Don't matter what time it is," Cuddy said. "There's no more drinks."

"You cuttin' us off, Frank?" Scott Parker asked.

"That's what I'm doin', Scott," Cuddy said. "When the boss calls for us, we're gonna have to be sober, not drunk."

"This town got a whorehouse?" Stokes asked.

"Sure does," Cuddy said. He decided not to tell them that Lincoln Town owned it. If he did, they'd be over there looking for a free poke—or, at least, a half-priced one.

"Where are we supposed to sleep?" Witt asked. "We ain't checked into a hotel."

"I got a place for you to sleep."

"Hell with that," Stokes said, standing up and swaying drunkenly, "I'm goin' to the whorehouse, get my ashes hauled."

"Rex," Cuddy said, "you're way too drunk to get yourself hauled."

Stokes grabbed his crotch and said, "I'm always ready—" then stopped and looked down at himself with a disappointed look on his face.

The other men started to laugh, except for Feathers, who had his eye on the back door because he thought he saw something—and then suddenly, the door from the saloon burst open, a split second before the back door did the same.

FORTY-TWO

The only way Clint could think of avoiding gunplay was to get the drop on Cuddy and his men. He had to depend on Giles for information about the saloon, and whether or not there was a back door. When they reached the saloon, Clint told Giles to go to the back, count to twenty, and then come in. As Clint approached the back room from inside the saloon, he knew that if he busted through this inside door, and there was no back door or, for some reason, Giles didn't come in at the same time, he was going to be facing five men alone.

And, of course, when you got the drop on someone, they had to be smart enough to know it . . .

Feathers saw the back door open as he stood up and went for his gun.

"Don't—" Clint shouted. He had gotten a description of Feathers from Giles, because he wanted to be sure to key in on the man.

Not only did Feathers freeze, but everyone else did, too. Clint had them covered from the front, while Giles had them from the back.

Cuddy eyed Baron Giles and said, "Hey, Baron."

"Frank."

Cuddy turned his head and looked at Clint.

"What's this about?"

"Louisa."

"The old dead whore? What about her?"

"Did you kill her?" Clint asked.

"Some old dead slag?" Cuddy smirked.

"It's about Juliet Fuller, too. Did you kill her?"

"I never touched her," Cuddy said.

"Town didn't tell you to kill her so he could take over her business?" Clint asked.

"Never said a word," Cuddy said. "The only person I'm waitin' for him to give me the word on is you, Adams."

"Adams?" Feathers asked. "Who is this man, Frank?"

"This is the famous Clint Adams, Theo," Cuddy said.

"Adams?" Stokes repeated drunkenly. "You mean, the goddamned Gunsmith?"

"That's right, Rex," Cuddy said. "The goddamned Gunsmith himself."

Suddenly, three men were glaring at Clint drunkenly. He noticed that Feathers and Cuddy seemed sober.

"Better get control of your boys, Frank," Clint said. "One of them goes for their gun, you're all dead."

"Two against five?" Cuddy asked. "And Baron, there, is an undertaker, not a gunny."

"I understand he shoots better than you," Clint said.

"Yeah, at targets," Cuddy said derisively. "He ain't never shot a man."

"There's always a first time."

Theo Feathers was watching Adams. If he could get the three drunks to draw first and attract Adams's attention, he knew he could take him. If Cuddy was right about the undertaker, then Adams was as good as dead.

Clint could see Feathers's mind working. The other three were just eyeing him and licking their lips. Cuddy was watching Giles. Feathers, however, was thinking.

That alone made him the dangerous one.

Cuddy thought that he and Feathers could take Clint Adams easily. All he needed to do was get Stokes and the other drunks to take care of Giles.

And what the hell was Adams talking about, accusing him of killing Juliet Fuller? He'd never laid a hand on the woman. Sure, he'd snapped the old whore Louisa's neck. She deserved it for slapping him. He'd followed her, taken care of her—the shocked look on her face was priceless—and then left town to go and meet Feathers and the others.

Maybe that's the key, he thought. *Unnerve the old gunman.* The Gunsmith couldn't be nearly as fast as he'd been years ago. He must have lost a step or two.

"Sure," he said, finally, "I killed the old bag. She deserved it. She was a waste of good air."

"Cuddy, I'm going to ask you and your friends to put your guns on the table."

"You boys want to put your guns on the table?" Feathers asked. "Or make a name for yourselves?"

"That's a bad move, Feathers," Clint said. "Don't get them all riled up. They'll only get killed."

Suddenly, the eyes of all five gunmen were on Clint Adams.

In the back of the room Baron Giles felt left out. Thanks to what Cuddy had said all five men had dismissed him.

They were all looking at Clint, all dreaming of making a reputation for themselves.

Too bad, he thought. *That would be their undoing.*

Of course, first he had to fire his gun at another human being, which he had never done before—but he could do it.

He knew he could.

Clint knew trouble was coming, and he hoped that Baron Giles was up to the task. It looked as if all five men were going to try drawing on him. He was going to have to take Feathers first and then Cuddy—but he recalled what Giles had said about Feathers, about him rushing his shots.

Cuddy first, he decided, then Feathers.

At least, he hoped it was the right decision.

FORTY-THREE

It was Stokes. He was the drunkest of them all, and all he saw was the Gunsmith standing in the doorway—an opportunity he could not pass up. He was just too drunk to think about the consequences of what he was about to do.

He went for his gun and Clint ignored him.

Baron Giles saw the man go for his gun and knew what he had to do. Clint was going to be watching Feathers and Cuddy, not the other men. That wasn't the plan, but then the plan had not been for all five men to ignore him. And he had no voice. The way things played out, Baron Giles shot his first man in the back . . .

Stokes staggered as Giles's shot struck him in the center of his back. The other drunks drew, as did Feathers and Cuddy.

Clint shot Cuddy first. He had to. The man had a good move and he'd be taking too much of a chance by leaving him for later. He shot him in the chest and hoped that it wouldn't kill him instantly . . .

* * *

The shock hit Cuddy before the pain. The shock of not
having even gotten a shot off. The Gunsmith was that
damned good! Before he knew it, he was on his back, trying to get his breath. *A doctor*, he thought, *maybe a doctor could save him* . . .

Feathers drew and fired a shot at Clint, but it went wide. It
didn't miss completely, though, taking a chunk out of
Clint's left arm, but he had to ignore that. The second
shot Clint fired hit Feathers in the chest and exploded his
heart . . .

Giles fired again and again. The other two drunks turned to
face him, so he was able to avoid shooting them in the
back. Even though his heart was racing, he remained calm.
As the men turned, he shot them each twice, and they went
down.

   Suddenly, the room was quiet and he and Clint were
the only two standing. He thought that the five men had
not been able to get off a shot when he saw the blood on
Clint's arm.

Clint walked around the room, blood dripping from his
arm as he checked each man in turn to be sure they were
dead. They all were—except Frank Cuddy. He was lin-
gering.

   "I need a doctor," he said to Clint.

   "Yeah, I'll get you a doctor, Frank," Clint said. "First
tell me, did you kill Juliet Fuller?"

   "No."

   "Did Town?"

   "I . . . don't . . . know . . ."

"Do you know—" Clint said, then stopped as he saw the life go out of Frank Cuddy's eyes.

He stood up, and Giles came over next to him.

"You did real good, kid."

"You think he was tellin' the truth?"

"He was dying," Clint said. "He was telling the truth."

"I don't see Lincoln Town killin' her," Giles said.

"I know," Clint said. "Men like that don't do their own killing."

"Then if neither of them killed Miss Fuller, who did?"

"We still have to find that out."

"You could use a doctor," Giles said.

Clint looked down at his arm and said, "Yeah, I guess I could."

FORTY-FOUR

Clint walked into Judge King's office the next morning with his left arm bandaged, and his right hand holding the brief Ray Olson had written. Sheriff Sheldon with was with Clint. Clint had spent the night at the whorehouse even though Frank Cuddy was dead. Deputy Evans had taken up a position at a window in one of the houses, using his badge to make the people let him in. Clint had spotted him and sent him home. Ginger had insisted on sleeping with Clint, in case he needed help with his arm during the night.

"What is the meaning—"the judge blustered, standing up behind his desk.

"Here's the brief you asked for," Clint said. "I expect you to rule quickly. If not, you'll be talking to some federal marshals and a federal judge. I don't know how scared you are of Lincoln Town, but after today he won't be a factor in this town. His pet killer is already dead, and I'm going to see Town next."

"But—" the judge started, then stopped himself. He sat back down, deflated.

"The sheriff is going to wait here for you to draw up

an order for Lincoln Town to vacate Juliet Fuller's business and to stay away."

Clint had already told Ginger that he was giving the business to her. He remembered their conversation.

"Can you do that?" she had asked.

"I'm going to do it," he had said. "Don't worry about it."

She had clasped her hands together and had said, "The first thing I'm gonna do is fire Regina."

"I don't think she'll be around to get fired," Clint had told her, but didn't explain.

Clint cut his musings short and turned to the sheriff. "Thanks for doing this, Sheldon."

"Time I did somethin' right," the lawman said.

"And thanks for letting me see Town on my own."

The sheriff shrugged and said, "That's the way you want it."

"Yes," Clint said, "it is."

When Clint came out of the building, Baron Giles was waiting for him.

"Going to the Pat Hand?"

"I am."

"Want some company?"

"Why not? You earned the right."

As they walked, Giles asked, "You figure out who killed Juliet Fuller?"

"I think so."

"Who?"

"Regina. She's the only one who really benefited, besides Lincoln Town."

"Do you think she did it for him?"

"No," Clint said, "I think he saw an opportunity after

Juliet was dead and moved in. Regina didn't expect that, but she had to put up with it."

"Where is she now?"

"At the house," Clint said. "I told my theory to the sheriff and he likes it. He's going to pick her up later."

"So what's left to do?" Giles asked.

"Just this," Clint said, stopping in from of the Pat Hand. "To tell Lincoln Town he has no rights to Juliet's business, and to suggest to him that it would be healthy for him to leave town."

"You think he'll do it?"

"By now he's heard the story of you and me killing five of his men," Clint said. "I think he'll see it my way. But I do have a job for you."

"What's that?"

"While I'm talking to him," Clint said, "stand behind me and look mean, like a killer."

Baron Giles smiled and said, "I'll give him my under-taker look. It'll be the last time I use it."

Watch for

ACE IN THE HOLE

316th novel in the exciting GUNSMITH series
from Jove

Coming in April!

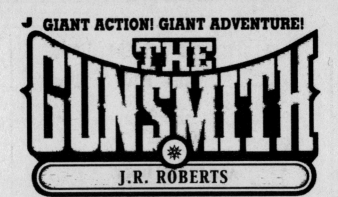

♦ GIANT ACTION! GIANT ADVENTURE!

THE GUNSMITH

J.R. ROBERTS

LITTLE SURESHOT AND THE WILD WEST SHOW
(GUNSMITH GIANT #9)
9780515138511

DEAD WEIGHT
(GUNSMITH GIANT #10)
9780515140286

RED MOUNTAIN
(GUNSMITH GIANT #11)
9780515142068

THE KNIGHTS OF MISERY
(GUNSMITH GIANT #12)
9780515143690

penguin.com

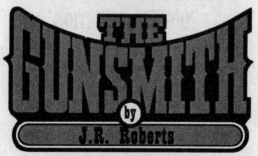

GIANT-SIZED ADVENTURE FROM AVENGING ANGEL LONGARM.

BY TABOR EVANS

2006 GIANT EDITION

LONGARM AND THE OUTLAW EMPRESS
978-0-515-14235-8

2007 GIANT EDITION

LONGARM AND THE GOLDEN EAGLE SHOOT-OUT
978-0-515-14358-4

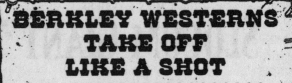

BERKLEY WESTERNS TAKE OFF LIKE A SHOT

- LYLE BRANDT
- PETER BRANDVOLD
- JACK BALLAS
- J. LEE BUTTS
- JORY SHERMAN
- ED GORMAN
- MIKE JAMESON

Don't miss the best Westerns from Berkley.

penguin.com